"TAKE IT E

"I can put a line of slug like a punch machine."

I didn't make the obvious retort. My throat was busy resisting the nausea that clenched my stomach.

It may have been the slick of blood on the floor where my foot had slipped. It may have been the half-naked man in the corner, with the dead, swollen face. It may have been the woman who lay on the table, the lamp shining full on the bloody towel which wrapped her face . . .

"Pretty, isn't it?" Garland said. "You see what happens to the boys and girls that buck our organization."

BLUE CITY
by
Ross Macdonald

"As tough as they come!"

BLUE CITY

Ross Macdonald

BANTAM BOOKS · TORONTO · NEW YORK · LONDON

*This low-priced Bantam Book
has been completely reset in a type face
designed for easy reading, and was printed
from new plates. It contains the complete
text of the original hard-cover edition.*
NOT ONE WORD HAS BEEN OMITTED.

🐥

BLUE CITY

*A Bantam Book / published by arrangement with
Alfred A. Knopf, Inc.*

PRINTING HISTORY

*Knopf edition published August 1947
Bantam edition published October 1958*
2nd printing November 1958   3rd printing ..October 1968
*4th printing ..October 1968
New Bantam edition published February 1974*

Published simultaneously in the United States and Canada

*Bantam Books are published by Bantam Books, Inc. Its trade-
mark, consisting of the words "Bantam Books" and the por-
trayal of a bantam, is registered in the United States Patent
Office and in other countries. Marca Registrada. Bantam
Books, Inc., 666 Fifth Avenue, New York, New York 10019.*

PRINTED IN THE UNITED STATES OF AMERICA

BLUE
CITY

Chapter 1

All the time you've been away from a town where you lived when you were a kid, you think about it and talk about it as if the air there were sweeter in the nostrils than other air. When you meet a man from that town you feel a kind of brotherhood with him, till the talk runs down and you can't remember any more names.

The city started sooner than I expected it to. In ten years it had crawled out along the highway, covering new farms with the concrete squares of suburban developments. On both sides of the highway I could see the rows of little frame houses, all alike, as if there were only one architect in the city and he had a magnificent obsession.

"It won't be long now," the transport driver said. He yawned over the wheel, keeping his eyes on the road. "I don't need any dago red to put me to sleep tonight."

"You live here?"

"I got a room in a boardinghouse at this end. You could call it living, I guess."

"Don't you like the town?"

"It's all right if you don't know any better places." He spat through his open window into the current of air that the truck's movement made, and a fine spray blew across the back of my neck. "I call Chicago home. That's where my wife is."

"That makes the difference."

"You married?"

"No," I said. "I'm traveling on my own."

"Looking for a job, eh?"

"That's right."

"You shouldn't have any trouble here. Matter of

1

fact, we need helpers down at the depot right now. Half the time I have to load my own truck. You strong enough?"

"Yeah, I'm strong enough. But that's not the kind of a job I was thinking about."

"Pretty good pay. Seventy cents an hour. You can't do better than that around here."

"Maybe I can. I've got connections."

"You have?" He gave me a quick look. I wasn't looking so good. I hadn't shaved or washed that day, and my clothes had been slept in.

He must have decided I was lying. He said with broad irony: "Oh well, in that case," and stopped talking to me.

The highway had changed into the east end of the main street, half residential and half business. Neighborhood grocery stores, coal yards, gas stations, cheap taverns, big old rundown houses, a few churches with blank embarrassed faces. I couldn't remember the buildings ahead of time, but nearly everything was familiar once I saw it. I caught a whiff of the rubber factories on the south side, corrupting the spring night like an armpit odor. I watched the suppertime crowds on the street, looking for someone I might remember.

The driver applied the brakes, and the truck came to a stop at the curb.

"I'll let you out here, bud. I can't take you down to the depot." He nodded toward the "No Riders" sticker on the windshield. "But in case your connections don't pan out, you want to come down there. It's on Masters Street."

"Thanks. And thanks for the ride."

I hoisted my canvas suitcase from under my feet and climbed down out of the cabin. The big truck moved away and left me standing on the curb.

I walked a couple of blocks in the direction the truck had taken, but I was in no hurry to go anywhere. The excitement I had felt on coming back to the city had worn off already. Men and women passed me going both ways, but they were nobody I knew. A policeman gave me a sharp glance. I realized that I must look like a bum, and the realization made me feel like one. I began to wonder for the first time that day if my connections in the town were worth anything. Perhaps they didn't even exist any more.

I passed a new apartment building whose windows were like holes in a box of light. Through one of them I caught a glimpse of a man and woman dancing to the radio, holding each other close. It was enough to bring back the feeling of loneliness that I had been having off and on for years. I wanted to know every room in every apartment in that building I had never seen before, and call everyone who lived there by his first name. At the same time I wished I had the power to destroy the building and everybody in it.

I hadn't had a fight for a long time, and I was spoiling for one.

Across the street a neon sign said: "Schlitz Beer on Draught," and I crossed to it. The plate-glass window of the tavern was half-curtained, but I could see over the curtain. It was a big square room full of wooden chairs and tables, with a bar at the back. In the cold yellow light of the fly-specked ceiling lamps, I could see that the tables were scarred by carved initials and the charred grooves left by untended cigarettes. The place was almost empty, and the few people that were there didn't look as if they'd make me feel out of place.

I went inside and sat on a stool at the bar. The bartender paid no attention to me. He was busy being a character for the benefit of a couple of other customers, a peroxide blonde and a henna redhead at the other end of the bar. The girls were sitting one on each side of a big young man in a topcoat made of imitation llama.

"So you want another drink," the bartender said with a wide cruel smile. "You think I got nothing better to do than give you another drink. Don't you know by this time of night all I can think about is my feet? My feet are killing me."

"Is that a promise?" the peroxide blonde said in a shrill, peroxide-blonde voice. The women giggled, and the man between them hugged them, one under each arm.

"The way you talk," the bartender said, "the way you talk, you'd think I get paid money to stand here and feed you characters whisky—when all the time my feet are killing me."

He was gray-headed and massive. His belly hung out over his belt and swayed like a huge bosom when he moved.

"You should try reducing, Henry," the blonde said. "Take some of that weight off your feet."

"Okay, okay," the bartender said. "You asked for it and you'll get it. But I warn you this bar whisky is the lousiest stuff this side of the sewer farm." He poured three shots out of an unlabeled bottle and set them on the bar.

"You should know, Henry," the blonde said.

"It's mother's milk to me," Henry said.

I rapped on the bar with a quarter.

"Somebody's getting impatient," Henry said. "When somebody gets impatient that makes me nervous. When I get nervous I'm no damn good for anything at all."

"A bottle of beer," I said.

"Look at my hand," Henry said. "It's trembling like a leaf." He held out a big gray hand and smiled down at it. "Beer, you say?"

"If this place is still in business."

He took a bottle out of the cooler, uncapped it, and shuffled along the bar towards me.

He looked at me with potential dislike. "What's the matter, you got no sense of humor?"

"Sure, but I checked it in another town. Go right on being sidesplitting for your friends."

"You're a stranger in town, aren't you? Maybe you just don't know how we talk around here."

"I'm learning fast."

"You can't learn too fast."

"Do you serve glasses with your beer? I'll have one."

"Olive or maraschino?"

"Just dip your thumb in it when you pour it."

"Pour it yourself."

I picked up my bottle and glass and sat down at a table against the wall. An old man with a glass of beer in front of him was facing me at the next table. There was a shag of beard on his face, shading from pure white on his cheeks and upper lip to iron gray on his flabby neck. When I had poured my beer and raised my glass to my lips, he raised his glass and winked at me.

I smiled back before I drank, and regretted it a minute later when he got up and moved towards my table. A shapeless brown overcoat hung about his body, and he walked like a sack of rags. He slumped into the other chair, rested his moth-eaten arms on the table, and leaned towards me with a sweet, dirty smile, which showed no teeth. He smelled of beer and age.

"It didn't used to be like this," he said. "But after all, life begins at sixty-five."

"Are you sixty-five?"

"Sixty-six. Yeah, I know I look older, but those strokes I had take it out of a man. The first one gave me a hell of a jolt, but it didn't hurt me any except that it slowed me down. But the second one was a dandy. I still can't use my left hand, probably never will be able to again."

"You've got funny reasons for saying that life begins at sixty-five."

"Sweet Cæsar, those aren't my reasons! It's for different reasons entirely that my life began at sixty-five. That was when I qualified."

"Qualified for what? Voting?"

"Qualified for the old-age pension, son. Ever since then I've been my own boss. No more getting pushed around, no more licking asses, not for me! Nobody can take that pension away from me."

"It's a great thing," I said.

"It's a wonderful thing. It's the most wonderful thing that ever happened to me in my life."

He finished his beer and I ordered him another.

"Who was your boss before you got the pension?"

"Can you imagine what they did to me?" the old man said. "And that was when I couldn't walk yet after my second stroke. They put me out in the county poor-house, with nobody to look after me except my chums out there. They said all the hospitals were full. I still have some of the bedsores I got then. And then they weren't going to give me my old-age pension, even after I qualified."

"What was the matter?"

"You see, son, I couldn't prove my age. You'd think if they took one look at me they could see how old I am, but that wasn't good enough. I was born on a farm and my daddy never registered my birth, so I couldn't get a birth certificate. I would've been up the creek without a paddle, if it hadn't been for Mr. Allister. He got my case investigated and people to swear to me, and everything turned out jake. Now I got me a little place of my own under the stairs at the warehouse, and nobody can say boo to me."

Two men came in and sat down at a table near us. One was short and broad. He wore a limp cloth cap and a decayed leather windbreaker. The other was tall and very thin, his face a vague triangle with the apex pointed down. He took a mouth organ out of the pocket of his shiny blue suit coat and blew a few dreamy notes. His companion drummed on the table with cracked dirty knuckles and looked stonily ahead.

"Who is this Allister?" I asked the old man.

"You don't know who Mr. Allister is? You haven't been around here long, have you? Mr. Allister is the Mayor of this town."

"And he helped you with your pension? He must be a pretty good egg."

"Mr. Allister is the finest man in this town."

"Things have changed around here," I said. "It used to be that J.D. Weather was the man to go to when you needed help like that. He used to have a line-up at his office every morning."

"J.D. Weather got killed before I had my second stroke. Let me see, that was two years ago this coming June. You used to live in this town, eh?"

"J.D. Weather got killed?"

"Yeah, about two years ago. Excuse me."

"Wait a minute. How did he get killed?" I put my hand on his arm, which felt like a bone wrapped in rags.

"He just plain got killed," the old man said impatiently. "Somebody shot him and he died."

"For Christ's sake! Who shot him?"

"You got to let me go, son. I been drinking beer."

I let go of his arm and he shuffled away to the men's room. The blonde and the redhead and their joint property in imitation llama had drifted away to other bars. The short man and the tall man finished their draught beers and wandered into the men's room. Now the room was deserted except for the bartender, who was wiping glasses and paying no attention to me. The ugly, empty room was one of a long series of lonely bars in towns I didn't know. If J.D. Weather was dead, this town was going to be as lonely as the rest.

There was a low growl of men's voices from the lavatory. I couldn't make out any words but there was unpleasantness in the sound, which was emphasized a minute later by a muffled thud. I glanced at the bartender, but he was busy with his glasses.

Then somebody sobbed in the men's room. I got up and walked through the door. The old man was sitting on the dirty tile floor with his back to the wall. A bead of blood had fallen from one of his nostrils onto his white mustache. The tall mouth organist and his companion stood in the center of the small room, watching me. The old man's hat was on the floor near their feet.

The old man was crying. "They took my money," he sobbed. "Make them give me back my money."

"We ain't got his money," the short man said. "He called me a dirty name, so I gave him a slap."

"The lousy, bullying bastards!" the old man said. "They took my sixteen dollars."

"You shut up," said the tall man, taking a step towards him.

"Leave him alone," I said. "And give him back his money."

The tall man stayed where he was.

"Oh, yeah?" the short man said. His eyes were bright

blue, as hard and glistening as glass eyes. "You and who else is going to make me?"

"I'm getting tired waiting," I said. "Give him back his money."

"He didn't have no money," the short man said. "C'mon, Swainie, let's get the hell out of here."

I braced my heel on the doorjamb and swung as I moved into him. He ducked his jaw quickly, but my fist caught the bridge of his nose. He moved in on me and clinched me around the waist with his round head under my right arm. "Get him from behind, Swainie," he said.

Before Swainie could circle me I backed into the closed door. I worked on the short man's arms but couldn't break his hold. Swainie came within range and I caught him on the ear with a backhanded left. The old man got to his feet and grabbed Swainie from behind with his one good arm. Swainie slammed him back against the wall, and the old man sat down on the floor again.

Meanwhile I had found the short man's belt. He was as squat and heavy as a sack of coal, but I strained him off the floor as Swainie came in again. When his legs were higher than his head, he let go of my waist. Then I threw him at Swainie.

One of his heavy work boots struck Swainie in the face and Swainie fell backwards onto the floor. The short man landed sprawling, rolled once to the far wall, and whirled like a terrier on his hands and knees. Before his hands were off the floor I hit him with an uppercut that had traveled three feet through the air. His head snapped back against the wall and he lay down on the floor, his open eyes looking more than ever like glass eyes. I was starting to breathe hard.

"You're pretty good," the old man said. I looked at him and saw that he wasn't sobbing any more.

"You're not so bad yourself. I saw you try to take on the big fellow. Which one got your money?"

"The short one. I think he put it in the breast pocket of his windbreaker."

I found the money and gave it to him. "Is there a phone in the bar?"

"Yeah."

"Then go and phone the police. I'll stay here and keep 'em quiet."

He looked at me in surprise, and chewed his blood-stained mustache. "Phone the police?"

"They robbed you, didn't they? They should be behind bars."

"Maybe so," the old man said. "But these fellows have an in with the police."

"You know them?"

"I've seen 'em around town. I think the cops brought 'em in for strikebreakers two years ago. They been here ever since."

"What kind of a police force does this town have, anyway?"

"That kind."

"Look." I found a nickel in my pocket and gave it to him. "Go and phone yourself a taxi and get out of here." He went out.

The short man was coming to. His head rolled on the floor and his eyes focused. He saw me and sat up.

"Stand up," I said. "Pour some water on your friend's face. I couldn't be bothered with him."

"You'll be sorry, fella. You don't know what you just been messin' with."

"Shut up or I'll hit you again! With both hands."

"Tough, eh?"

My left split his upper lip and my right closed his left eye. "See what I mean?"

He leaned against the wall and put his black-grained hands over his damaged face. I went out to the bar, where the old man was sitting on a stool.

"I like your class of clientele," I told the bartender.

"You back? I don't recall as how we sent you a gilt-edged invitation."

"If the comic in the lavatory doesn't come to in another five minutes, you better send for the police ambulance."

"You been fighting?" He looked at me with hypocritical disapproval. "We don't allow any roughhouse stuff around here."

"I didn't notice you raising a howl when this old guy got hit. What's your cut?"

"One more crack like that out of you!" the bartender yelled.

A car honked softly in front of the tavern, and the old man slid off his stool.

"Save it," I told the bartender.

The old man was at the door, and I called to him to wait a minute. "Do you live far?"

"Just a few blocks."

"Fifty cents should cover it." I gave him two quarters.

"You're a good boy, son."

"I just happen to like fighting. What's your name?"

"McGinis."

"If those characters give you any more trouble, let me know. I'll be staying at the Weather House, I guess. My name's John Weather. Better stay away from here, though."

"You mean the Palace Hotel? That's the old Weather House."

"Yeah, I suppose they would change its name."

The taxi honked mildly again, and the old man turned away. "Wait a minute," he said again. "What did you say your name was?"

"John Weather."

"You any relation to J.D. Weather that I was telling you about?"

"That's right."

"Is that a fact?" the old man said. He got into his taxi and rode away.

Chapter 2

They had changed more than the name of the Weather House. The Palace Hotel had revolving doors instead of the big oak doors with the brass knobs that I remembered. The dim old lobby with the tobacco-colored, tobacco-smelling leather chairs had been cleaned out and redecorated. It was a bright, female sort of place now, with indirect lighting and new, colored chesterfields, and there were no old men sitting in it. The ground-floor poolroom where J.D. once played Willie Hoppe had been changed into a cocktail lounge with dark blue women painted on the walls. I looked past the bare shoulders of a couple of floozies at the door of the cocktail lounge and saw that it was doing a good business, which included the high-school trade. I couldn't help wondering where the money from the business was going.

I crossed the lobby to the room clerk's desk. It bore a little wooden sign which said "Mr. Dundee." Mr. Dundee looked at my rain-stained fedora, my beard-blackened chin, my dirty shirt, my canvas bag, my old field boots. I looked at Mr. Dundee's wig-brown hair, carefully parted in the exact center of his egg-shaped skull. I looked at his fat, laundered little face and his dull little eyes, his very white hard collar and his pale-blue tie which was held in place by a gold-plated initialed clasp.

I began to look at each of the eight manicured fingers with which he daintily clasped the inside edge of the desk.

"What can we do for you?" he said, delicately omitting the "sir."

"Single without bath. I never take a bath. Do I?"

11

He raised his thin eyebrows and blinked. "That will be two dollars and a half."

"I usually pay when I check out of a hotel. Who runs this place?"

"Mr. Sanford is the owner," said Mr. Dundee. "Two dollars and a half, please."

I took out a roll that looked bigger than it was and gave him three ones. "Keep the change."

"The salaried officers of this hotel do not accept tips."

"Excuse me," I said. "You remind me of a butler I once had. He died of chagrin on his fiftieth birthday."

Mr. Dundee placed my key and my change flatly on the counter and said distantly: "Six seventeen."

Just before he closed the door of 617, the bellboy looked at me sideways with a fifty-cent smile. "Anything else I can get you, sir? There's some pretty nice stuff in this town."

"Alcoholic or sexual?"

"Both. Anything you want."

"Just buy me a piece of privacy. But don't bring it up yourself."

"Yes, sir. Excuse me, sir." The door clicked behind him.

I stripped to the waist, washed from there up, shaved, and put on a clean shirt. I counted my money and found that I still had sixty-three dollars and some change from the last hundred dollars of my mustering-out pay. I weighed a hundred and eighty stripped and was almost as fast as a welter-weight. It was twenty minutes past seven.

I went down the fire stairs to the broadcasting studio on the third floor. It occupied the same suite as it had ten years before, but the partition between the anteroom and the broadcasting chamber had been torn out, and a plate-glass window substituted. On the other side of the window, a dried-up little man in a swallow-tailed coat was talking into the microphone. It took me a moment to realize that the great deep voice coming through the loudspeaker in the anteroom belonged to the little man at the mike.

"Fearful One," the great voice said, and the little man's lips followed the syllables like a ventriloquist's dummy. "Fearful One, you stand at the crossroads of your destiny, and I believe you possess the spiritual power to sense that disturbing fact. But do not be alarmed by the slings and arrows of outrageous misfortune. I can help you, out of the power of my knowledge and the knowledge of my power. . . ."

A big young man in a gray suit was sitting at a table in the corner. I said to him: "Anybody in charge around here, or does the old gent just carry on by himself?"

"I happen to be the program director." He stood up and shook the wrinkles out of his sharply creased trousers. He looked as if he had just stepped out of a men's clothing store via a barbershop.

"In that case," I said, "maybe you can tell me who runs this station."

"I just told you I was the program director." His voice was as cultured as an uncultured voice ever gets to be. Already it contained a little whine of impatience and wounded vanity.

"But somebody pays your salary, which I trust is large."

"Who are you? I don't like your tone."

"Excuse me, I flunked out of the Juilliard School. But I was just asking for a little information in my crude way."

"Mrs. Weather owns the station, of course."

The big voice from the loudspeaker intoned: "That is my advice to you, Fearful One. Rear the child yourself. Bring up the little one in the ways of righteousness, and strive mightily to sustain yourself in worthiness for the noble career of motherhood. If you desire further advice and comfort from the seventh son of a seventh son, come to me in my office any day this week. Hours from ten in the morning till five in the afternoon."

I said loudly: "Mrs. Weather died five years ago."

"Please don't shout," the program director said. "Our soundproofing isn't very good. You must be thinking of

somebody else. I saw Mrs. Weather this afternoon, and
she was in perfect health."

"Did J.D. Weather marry again?"

"That's true, I did hear Mr. Weather had been married before. He remarried a few months before his
death."

"Is she running the hotel, too?"

"As a matter of fact, she isn't. It was sold to Mr.
Sanford."

"The rubber-company Sanford?"

"Right."

"He still lives in that big house on the north side,
doesn't he?"

"That's right. Now you'll have to excuse me." He
trotted silently across the carpet to the door of the
broadcasting chamber.

The loudspeaker was saying: "A genuine herbal rem-
edy, prepared according to the exact and exotic for-
mula of an ancient Oriental savant. This priceless medicine will cure or alleviate ailments of the heart, blood,
stomach, liver, and kidneys. It is helpful in treating dis-
eases of both men and women, and acts as a rare tonic
in cases of depleted energy and low spirits generally.
Just mail a dollar, plus a nominal fee of ten cents for
wrapping, to this station, and get your large introduc-
tory bottle of Novena."

The little man in the swallow-tailed coat moved
away from the microphone to the door, and the program director took his place. "You have just been listening to Professor Salamander, seventh son of a seventh son and purveyor of age-old wisdom." As the an-
nouncement continued, a record player played a few
bars of the "Barcarolle." Then the program director announced a half-hour of "Jazztime," and began to create
atmosphere with his voice.

I didn't like the atmosphere created by his voice, and
I went away. Professor Salamander and I rode the
same elevator down. His eyeballs were yellow. He
smelt strongly of whisky. He muttered to himself.

I had been there once or twice with my father, but I

remembered the location of Mr. Sanford's house only vaguely, so I took a taxi.

"You want me to let you off at the service entrance?" the driver said when we got there.

"Drive me up to the front door. I haven't got anything to sell. And wait for me. I won't be long."

The house, which had been built by Mr. Sanford's father, was a rambling white brick building with eighteen or twenty rooms. A grandiose and useless tower at each end of the façade gave it a feudal touch. Its grounds occupied a city block, and included a sunken garden, tennis courts, and a swimming pool, which kept Alonzo Sanford and his friends off the streets. Only when a strong and steady south wind was blowing, did the odor of the rubber factories reach Mr. Sanford's front yard.

A Negro maid in white collar and cap answered the doorbell.

"Is Mr. Sanford home?"

"I'm not sure. Who shall I say is calling, please?"

"Tell him John Weather. J.D. Weather's son."

She let me in and left me on a chair in the vestibule, holding my hat on my knees. After a moment she returned and took my hat. "Mr. Sanford will see you in the library."

When I came in, Mr. Sanford put down his open book on the wide arm of his chair and marked his place with his reading glasses. He didn't look ten years older, but I noticed that when he got up he leaned forward over his knees and pushed with his arms as well as his legs. He had on a silk lounging robe with a red velvet collar. He came towards me with his hand outstretched.

His face had thinned and dried, so that his smile was like carefully folded paper. "Johnny Weather, I do declare! This really calls for a drink. You look big enough to have a drink." He chuckled paternally.

"Maybe a short lemonade. I'm awfully big for my age."

He smiled again with all his scrupulously matched teeth. "Now let me see, what would your age be? I know I should be able to tell you, but when you're my age you don't number the years with such painstaking accuracy. Twenty or twenty-one?"

"Twenty-two," I said. "Old enough to inherit property."

He said: "Excuse me," rang the bell for the maid, and asked for drinks.

"Won't you please sit down? There, that's better. Believe me, I can understand a little bitterness on your part, Johnny. From your point of view it was sheer bad luck that your father remarried a few months before his unfortunate—demise."

"Who did he marry? Who killed him?"

"Do you mean to say you've never met your stepmother?"

"I never even heard of her before tonight. She's a stranger to me. There seems to have been practically a hundred per cent turnover in this town."

"I'm sure you'll find her quite a charming young woman. I've had relations with her on several occasions, business and otherwise, and I've found her consistently charming."

"How nice for both of you! I hear she sold you the hotel."

"As a matter of fact, she did. Mrs. Weather, and her business agent, Mr. Kerch, decided to cut down a bit on her holdings in real property. And I've had no reason to regret the investment."

"It's funny to hear you call this woman Mrs. Weather. My mother died five years ago."

"Yes, yes," said Mr. Sanford. "Most unfortunate."

The maid brought brandy highballs, and Mr. Sanford lit a cigar. "Your father tried to find you, you know," he went on. "What in the world happened to you, Johnny?"

"I moved around. I didn't like my father at that time, and I promised my mother I wouldn't go back to him. I lived in various parts of the country for a couple of years, and then the draft got me. The last year or two I've felt different about my father."

"Of course. It's hard to think ill of the dead."

"That's not the point. You see, I didn't know he was dead until tonight."

"You mean to say you weren't informed?"

"When was he killed?"

"Nearly two years ago. April of 1944, I believe it was."

"I was in England then. Nobody went to the trouble of letting me know."

"That is a crying shame."

"Who killed him?"

"The crime was never solved. We all did what we could. You must know that your father and I were quite close at one time. His death was a rude shock to me."

"It got you the Weather House. There can't be much of the town you don't own by now."

He sipped his highball and looked at me coldly over the rim of the glass. "As I said before, I can understand your being a little bitter, Johnny, inasmuch as your father's will cut you off without a cent. Still, I think it's unwise of you to insult your potential friends. I was prepared to be quite sympathetic towards you."

"Your sympathy isn't negotiable. It didn't do my father much good. And your little threat isn't very frightening. You can't browbeat me with money till I come asking you for something."

He leaned forward and his pale old eyes gave me a blank stare that tried to look candid. "You seem to have gotten some very strange notions into your head. I was under the impression that you came to me as an old friend of your father's." He paused and examined my unpolished field boots and my unpressed clothes. "Perhaps with some idea of asking me for assistance."

"I haven't asked anybody for anything in years."

"Quite. But your attitude strikes me as unnecessarily aggressive—"

"This is a rough town, Mr. Sanford. You know that—it's your town. Two years ago my father was killed in it. What happened to the investigation of his death?"

"I told you that the crime has remained unsolved. He was shot on the street and his assailant was never apprehended."

"Is the case still open, or was it dropped?"

"I'm afraid I can't tell you that. Why you should assume that I had anything to do with the investigation—"

"An important case wouldn't be dropped without your tacit approval."

We had finished our highballs. He put his glass down on the table with a slightly peremptory rap. "You have a curious conception of the function of a wealthy man in a modern democratic municipality. We are all under the law, Mr. Weather. We must all try to get along with our neighbors."

"J.D. used to try to, but one of his neighbors shot him on the street. Who handled the case?"

"Inspector Hanson, I believe. Ralph Hanson." He stood up, picked up his book, and put on his reading glasses. Now he looked more than ever like an exquisite old scholar who had abandoned the pleasures of the world.

"*The Theory of the Leisure Class* is a funny book for you to be reading."

He smiled his careful, crumpled smile. "Do you really think so? Veblen analyzes some of the illusions of my class very competently, I think. He helps me to be without illusions."

"There's one you'll never lose. Every man that's born rich brings it with him out of the nursery and holds on to it for the rest of his life—the illusion of his own superiority."

"You had a lot of money when you were a young boy, didn't you?" he said. "And I haven't observed that you are afflicted with an inferiority complex."

He rang the bell and the maid appeared to show me out.

"One more thing," I said. "This Mrs. Weather got all my father's property. Who's next in line?"

"You are, I believe. But Mrs. Weather is both young and, so far as I have heard, healthy."

He didn't offer his hand again. I left him standing with his finger in Veblen, neck-deep in conspicuous consumption.

Chapter 3

Inspector Ralph Hanson lived in the new east end, in one of the mass-produced houses I had seen when I first came into town. My taxi driver's flashlight found the number, which I had looked up in the telephone directory, and I asked him to wait again. It wasn't a big house but it was well kept, surrounded by carefully trimmed shrubbery and a lawn as smooth as a putting green. I climbed the veranda steps and knocked on the door with the ornamental iron knocker.

A middle-aged woman, whose figure had never recovered from childbearing, opened the door and smiled at me uncertainly. I noticed a tricycle beside the door and a doll carriage in the hall. I asked her if Inspector Hanson was home.

"Ralph's in his workshop in the basement. You can just go down there if you want to."

"I came here on business," I said. "Perhaps you'd better call him up."

The screeching of a plane on wood, which I had been hearing through the floor, stopped when she called down the stairs: "Ralph! There's a young man here to see you."

Hanson was rolling down his shirt sleeves when he came up, and the hairy backs of his hands were still dusted with little shavings. He was a tall man with a long, sour face and quick, green eyes. He stood in the hallway for a moment brushing off his hands.

"Oh, Ralph," his wife said in an indulgent whine. "I asked you to be careful about bringing your dirt up here."

"It isn't dirt," he said sharply. "It's good, clean wood."

"It's just as hard to clean up as dirt," she stated, and disappeared into the back of the house.

He looked me up and down and assigned me a mental classification that I could guess from his abrupt: "And what can I do for you, sir?"

I said: "A couple of years ago you investigated the murder of J.D. Weather. Is that correct?"

"That's correct. I was in charge of the case."

"Do you know who killed him?"

"No. I came to a dead end. We never caught the murderer."

"Does that mean you couldn't or you didn't?"

He looked at me with hostility. His thin lips drew back from his teeth in an involuntary grimace, and I saw they were yellow and long like hound's teeth. "I don't like that crack. Just what is your interest in the case?"

"I'm his son."

"Why didn't you say so, then? Come in and sit down."

He waved me ahead of him into the living-room and switched on the ceiling light. It was a small room, too full of overstuffed furniture, with French-type windows on two sides and a fireplace containing a gas heater on the third. He placed me on a mohair chesterfield and sat down in a matching armchair facing me. The room was as homelike as the display window of an installment furniture store, but my host was trying to look more friendly. His long face creased in a smile that might have been mistaken for a look of pain.

"So you're John, eh? I remember when you used to tag around with J.D. when you were a kid. I was on a motorcycle then."

"You've been doing all right," I said.

He looked around the room with grim complacence. "Yeah, they promoted me to Inspector last year."

"Who did?"

"The police board. Who do you think?"

"Not, I take it, for your work on my father's murder?"

He leaned forward and spoke rapidly with an almost

neurotic excitement: "You'll get nothing by coming around and throwing that in my teeth. I liked J.D. I worked hard on the case."

"Everybody liked J.D., with the possible exception of my mother. And somebody who shot him on the street. And maybe a few other people who covered up for the man that shot him."

"I don't know what kind of stories you've been hearing," Hanson said.

"I haven't been hearing a damn thing. That's the trouble. I don't even know what happened to him."

"You just told me."

"I told you what I heard from an old man in a bar. How was he murdered?"

"You want it in detail?"

"As much as you can give me."

He sat back in his chair and made an arch of his fingers. His story came as pat and clear as rehearsed testimony:

"He was shot at approximately 6:35 in the evening on April 3, 1944, as he was on his way home from the hotel. The shooting occurred one block north of Main Street on Cleery, near the corner of Cleery and Mack. Two shots were fired, almost simultaneously, according to witnesses. Both shots struck him in the head and pierced his brain, and he died immediately."

"Didn't anybody see the killer?"

"That's one of the things that stymied me. Nobody did. It was an ambush killing, well planned ahead of time, and the killer had his getaway prepared. Remember the old Mack Building?"

"No. Tell me about it."

"It's on the corner of Cleery and Mack, with entrances on both streets. J.D. went past it every day about the same time on his way home from his office. The man who shot him must have known that, because he waited for him at a window on the second floor of the Mack Building. The window was about fourteen feet above street level. When J.D. came past, the killer leaned out of the window and shot him from above. At least that's the way I reconstructed it. It fits in with the path the bullets took."

"Whose window was it?"

"Nobody's. It was an empty office—used to be a dentist's office. We found out afterwards that somebody had broken into it. The door had been jimmied, and there were marks in the dust on one of the window ledges where somebody rested his arm."

"Fingerprints?"

"No. I told you it was well planned. The killer fired his two shots, put down the window, and beat it through the building and out the other entrance. By that time nearly all the offices were closed and there was hardly anybody in the building, so nobody saw him. Probably he had a car waiting for him at the Mack Street entrance. Anyway, he got clear away."

"And that's all you've been able to find out in two years?"

"One more thing. We recovered the murder weapon and traced it. It was an old Smith and Wesson revolver, and it's definitely the gun that fired the bullets that killed J.D. We found it in the sewer on Mack Street near the entrance to the Mack Building. Up to a certain point it was easy to trace. The daughter of the original purchaser, a man called Teagarden, sold it to Kaufman the secondhand dealer. Kaufman admitted buying it, but claimed that it was stolen from his store a couple of days before the murder."

"You investigated Kaufman?"

"Naturally. He's a shady customer all right, some kind of an anarchist or radical. He writes crazy letters to the newspapers. But he didn't kill your father. He was in his store at the time of the murder, and has two or three people to swear to it. It could be that he sold the gun to somebody and then to cover up he made up this story about a shoplifter. But it sounded to me as if he was telling the truth."

"I suppose you went into the matter of who stood to profit by J.D.'s death."

His long body wriggled uneasily against the cushions of his chair. "I did what I could. Mrs. Weather was the only one who profited directly. She inherited his money and property. But there isn't any other reason to suspect her. You know that as well as I do."

"The hell I do. Just who is this woman?"

"Don't you know her? I thought you'd probably be staying with her."

"Not if I can help it." I stood up and walked across the rug to the mantel. "I've never seen her, and what I've heard about her I don't like."

"Naturally you wouldn't like her. But she's a pretty nice kid. She's got a good deal of class."

"Where did she come from?"

"Chicago, I think. Anyway, your father brought her home from Chicago on one of his trips. She was his secretary for a while before he married her. From all I heard, she made him a good wife. The women in the town don't like her much, but you can expect that. They haven't got her class."

"I'll have to take a look at all that class. She still lives here?"

"Yeah, she just stayed on in J.D.'s house. It's her house now, of course."

"Do I know as much about the case now as you do?"

"I told you the main facts. Maybe I left out some of the details—"

"Such as who killed my father."

He stood up and faced me with bubbling anger in his narrow green eyes. "I told you a straight story. If you don't like it, you can shove it."

"I don't like it and I'm not going to shove it. I'd like to know if anybody warned you not to find out too much."

His lips drew back from his teeth again and his voice rasped: "I did my job and I told you what I knew. Now you can get out of my house."

I found his eyes with mine, stared hard, and stared him down. "You're acting nervous, Inspector Hanson. Tell me what's making you nervous and I'll get out."

"I'm not afraid of anybody, and if a snotnose like you thinks he can—"

"You could have the makings of an honest man, Hanson. You like good, clean wood. How do you put up with working on a dirty police force like the one in this town?"

He took a step towards me and glared in my face. He was a tall man, an inch or two taller than I, but lean and brittle. I could have broken him in two, but he didn't seem to be worrying about that: "One more crack out of you—"

"And you'll swing at me and I'll have to hurt you and you'll call your wagon and put me away in jail to rot."

"I didn't say that. But in this town you're going to talk yourself into trouble."

"If I talk myself into it, I'll fight my way out."

"I mean bad trouble," he said soberly. "Maybe you better drop the whole thing."

"The way you did? Are you trying to scare me the way somebody scared you?"

"Nobody scared me!" he shouted. "Get out!"

"So you really like this town the way it is. You like being a middling-big frog in a puddle of slime."

For a full half-minute he didn't say a word. His face twitched once or twice and became still. Finally he said: "You don't know what you're talking about. When a man's got a wife and kids and a house to pay for—"

"You want your kids to grow up in a place where the cops are as crooked as the crooks? You want them to find out that their old man is one of those cops, and getting along pretty nicely in a setup like that? It's funny you wouldn't want to clean the place up for your kids."

A bitter smile drew the corners of his mouth down. "I told you you didn't know what you were talking about, Weather. If this town needs cleaning up, your old man had a lot to do with it."

"Whatever the hell that means."

"It means that this town got its first real taste of corruption when J.D. moved in his slot machines thirty years ago. First, he bought himself into the police force so they wouldn't throw his slot machines out of town. Then, he bought himself into the municipal government so they wouldn't clean up the police force. And don't call me a liar, because I know what I'm talking about. I've had my cut."

I didn't want to believe it, but it sounded like the truth. It gave my stomach a queer twist. Except where women were concerned, I had always thought my father was the straightest man in the Middle West.

Chapter 4

Taxis were costing me more than I could afford, but I was in a hurry and the evening was slipping away. The driver took me straight down Main Street into the heart of town. The night streets were crowded with noisy couples, young girls in twos and threes looking for a pickup, boys and young men in threes and fours marching abreast and wearing bright ties like banners. Spring ran in the gutters like a swift, foul stream, and the people in the streets moved and regrouped in a slow, enormous Bacchic dance. We turned at the Palace Hotel and went up Cleery Street into the north side of town.

All the windows were dark on the second floor of the Mack Building, and there was no bronze plaque on the sidewalk where J.D. Weather had died.

Even his house looked the same, though it was smaller than I remembered. Nothing had changed, except that I couldn't walk in without knocking, and nobody there would be glad to see me. When I went up the front steps I had the feeling that I was about to do something I had often done before. I rang the bell and waited. The feeling went away before the door opened, and left me half-angry and half-embarrassed.

The porch light came on over my head, and the door opened on a chain. Through the opening I could see a four-inch section of a woman: carefully lacquered, upswept auburn hair, dark eyes in a pale face, a white neck rising from a low, plain neckline.

"Mrs. Weather?"

"Yes."

"I'd like to talk to you. I think you must be my stepmother."

27

She made a noise in her throat, a little chuckling gasp. "Are you John Weather?"

"Yes. May I come in?"

"Of course. Please do." She unhooked the chain and stepped back to open the door. "I shouldn't have kept you standing outside. But I'm alone in the house tonight, and you never know about night callers. This is the maid's night off."

"I know how you feel," I said, but I wasn't thinking of her. The old hall tree was gone, and the moose head was missing from over the door. The floor had been re-finished, and there was a new pastel rug on it. Ivory enamel made the staircase look unreal. Everything was too pale and neat.

"You used to live in this house, didn't you?" she said.

"I was just thinking of that. It's different."

"I hope you approve of the changes." Her tone was a subtle blend of arrogance and feminine cajolery.

Her voice interested me. It was a good voice, low, rich, and complex, with a more frankly female quality than perfect ladies allow themselves. I looked into her face and said: "There have been too many changes to generalize about, haven't there? Not that my opinion matters one way or the other."

She turned on her heel and walked to the door of the living-room. "Won't you come in and sit down and have a drink? We must have things to talk about."

I said: "Thank you," and followed her. If her breasts and her hips were her own, her figure was very hand-some. Even if they weren't, she had her legs, and the way she moved her body. In her dark silk dress she moved with the free, shining fullness and flow of a seal in water.

The face she leaned towards me, as we sat down fac-ing each other, was in contrast to her body. It had a bloodless kind of beauty, emphasized by her scarlet mouth, but it was thin and worried-looking. Her wide, dark eyes seemed to have drawn out and to hold all the life and energy of her face. Her bright hair stood above her pale face and neck like a curled, red flower on a stalk that the sun had missed.

She smiled nervously under my stare. "Do you think you've got my Bertillon measurements by now?"

"Excuse me. I'm naturally interested in my father's last wife."

"That's not a very chivalrous thing to say."

"My chivalry is my weakest point."

"That's true of your whole generation, isn't it? Or maybe you've been reading Hemingway or something."

"Don't start talking down like a stepmother. You haven't got much of a drop on me where age is concerned."

Her laugh came strangely out of her unmoving face. "Maybe I was wrong about your chivalry. But don't kid yourself. I belong to the lost generation. Which reminds me, I promised you a drink."

I said: "Who's been reading Hemingway now?" and looked around the room while she went to the bar in the corner. The bar had been J.D.'s idea, but the rest of the room had been remade. Thick, bright curtains at the windows, low, square-cut furniture placed in complicated geometric patterns on a desert expanse of polished floor, chaste walls and soft indirect lighting, which made the ceiling seem high and airy. The only old-fashioned survival was the pair of sliding doors which closed off the dining room. It was a beautiful room but it lacked life. Time and change had tiptoed away and left it breathless and still. I wondered if the rich, widowed body of the woman who had invented the room spent lonely nights.

She gave me a bourbon with a little soda and a lot of ice. Then she raised her glass and said: "Here's to chivalry." Her hands were white and well kept, but there was a little gathering and puckering of the flesh at the wrist. Perhaps I had been wrong about her age, but it couldn't be more than thirty-five.

"Here's to women that aren't dependent on it."

She looked at me for a moment and said slowly: "You're rather a nice boy."

"You're not exactly a typical stepmother. Or did I read too much Grimm in my formative years?"

"I doubt it. What are your plans, John?"

"It's a funny thing. I came here with the idea of asking J.D. for a job. I've been at a loose end since I got out of the army—"

"Didn't you know he was dead?"

"Not until today. You see, after my mother left him we never heard from him. I almost forgot I had a father. But I've been thinking about him the last couple of years in the army. I didn't try to get in touch with him, but I thought about him. So I finally decided to come and see him. I was a little late."

"You should have come before." She leaned forward to touch my knee, and I could see the single young line made by the separation of her breasts in the V of her neckline. "He often talked about you. You should have written, anyway."

"What did he say about me?"

She made the removal of her hand from my knee as definite a gesture as placing it there. "He loved you, and he wondered what had happened to you. He was afraid your mother would teach you to hate him."

"She did her best, but in the long run it didn't take. I can't say I blame her entirely."

"Don't you, really?"

"Why should I? He hated her for leaving him. He never tried to get in touch with us."

"Why did she leave him, Johnny?" Her way of speaking to me was moving through gradual stages of intimacy, and I felt a little crowded. "He never told me," she said.

So far, the conversation had gone all her way, and she had chosen the reminiscent and sentimental vein. I chose another: "Because he couldn't keep his hands off women."

She seemed neither shocked nor displeased. She leaned back in her low chair and stretched her arms over her head. Her live, stirring body in that still room was like a snake in a sealed tomb, fed by unhealthy meat. She said in a soft and questioning voice: "You

must have known your way around when you were
twelve."

She leaned her head against the back of the chair
and looked at the ceiling. Her body, stretched out before me, seemed lost in a dream of its own power and
beauty. I could have reached out and taken it, I
thought, like a ripe fruit from a tree. But then she was
my stepmother and that would be incestuous. Besides, I
hated her guts.

I said as casually as I could: "Just what happened to
J.D.?"

Her head came erect and her dark emotional eyes
looked at me. "He was shot down on the street. Nobody knows who did it. It was a hideous thing. I'm not
sure I can talk about it—even yet." Her voice broke.

"You must have loved him very much."

"I was mad about him," she said throatily. "He was
the man in my life." She was sitting straight up now.
Her white hands on the arms of the chair and her
crowning hair made her look like a tragic queen.

"Wasn't he a little old for you?"

She watched me for a moment and decided that I
meant nothing by it. "Some people thought so," she
said defiantly, "but I never did. Jerry had the secret of
eternal youth."

"If not eternal life. Property lasts, though. He left a
good deal of property, didn't he?"

I hadn't been feeding her the right lines and she
seemed a little confused. "What do you mean? He left
me well provided for, of course."

"That's fine. It must be almost as fine for you as if
he'd gone on living."

She regrouped her forces and fell back to her original lines of defense: "Johnny, you don't hate me, do
you? I hadn't even the slightest idea what was in his
will before he died. I know it's rough on you."

"He didn't die. He was shot. It was rough on him.
Have you an idea who shot him?"

"How should I know?" She made a face like a little
girl, pursing her lips in an artificial rosebud. "He must

have had enemies, Johnny. He had so many different business interests."

"You think it was assassination for business reasons, then? Who do you have in mind?"

The question frightened her. Her white face remained composed, but her whole body stiffened. "Why, nobody. I know so little about his business."

"Did you post a reward for the murderer?"

"No, I didn't. I was advised not to."

"Who advised you?"

"I don't remember. One of his friends, it must have been. They said the police wanted a chance to work on the case quietly."

"They worked quietly, all right. This case has closed up so quietly I feel as if I've gone deaf."

"I think the police did their best, Johnny. Inspector Hanson worked on it for weeks."

"Sewing it up at the seams, probably. Sealing it hermetically so no air would ever get in. Where were you when J.D. was shot, or is that part of the secret archives?"

I had given her cause for genuine anger, but she was doped by the histrionic emotion she had been feeding me. She covered her face with her hands and said brokenly between them: "How can you make such an utterly horrible insinuation? I was home helping the cook to prepare his dinner—a dinner he never ate."

The defensive unreality of her reactions was too much for me. I decided to play along with her and see where it got us: "I didn't really mean that, you know that. It's just that I haven't been able to find out anything, and it's getting me down."

She took her hands away and peered into my face with dry eyes. "I know. It got me down long ago. I've had two years of this dreadful uncertainty."

"About what, exactly?"

"About what happened to Jerry. And what might happen to me. I've been carrying on his business, you know."

"I heard you sold the hotel."

"Yes, I had to let it go." She seemed embarrassed.

"But I'm still running the Cathay Club, and the station. That used to be my work, you see. I've been in radio for years. Jerry hired me in the first place to look after his radio interests."

"What about the slot machines?"

"I keep out of that side of the business. They're not really a woman's field. I had to hire a business agent. He manages the Cathay Club, too."

"I suppose that's Kerch."

"Oh, do you know him?"

"Not yet," I said.

"If you'd like to meet him I could arrange it. Though I don't see what interest you'd have—"

"I'm interested in anybody that got anything out of J.D.'s death."

She looked at me uncertainly. "Surely you're not still interested in me—in that way?"

I stared frankly at her red mouth, let my stare drop to her full bosom and taut waist. "I'm interested in you in all sorts of ways."

"I was afraid for a while you were going to act like a stepson. But you're not talking like one now." She let her lips remain parted when she finished speaking. A little flicker of triumph danced in her eyes. She stood up and expanded her body. "Let me make you another drink."

"Thanks. I don't think I'll have another drink."

"You're not leaving again, so soon?" She spoke as she moved across the room.

"I've got a lot of things to do that won't wait. A lot of people to see."

She turned from the bar and faced me. Her right hand twisted a bracelet on her left wrist, almost as if she were clutching at herself for support. "What people?"

"Maybe you can make some suggestions. You know what I'm looking for."

She filled a double pony with bourbon and drank it quickly. "No, I can't offer any suggestions. I'm as much in the dark as you are. Don't you believe me?"

"Why should I?"

"But you've got to believe me." She recrossed the room towards me. Her arms hung straight down by her sides now, lending her body a queer, stealthy dignity.

I stood up and looked into her face. It was deceptively calm, like the frozen surface of a dark stream. In the bottom of her eyes I could see the shifting play of hidden currents, without being able to guess their meaning.

"If you want to see Kerch," she said rapidly, "I'll take you to him tomorrow."

"Do I need a formal introduction?"

"No, of course not. But you can't do anything tonight. It's getting late. You might just as well sit down and have another drink."

"Maybe it would suit you better if I waited till next year or the year after."

"What do you mean?"

"You seem very eager to have me do nothing at all. I'd expect you to have some interest in the matter of who killed your husband. Curiosity, anyway."

"You don't understand, Johnny. You can't understand how hard it's been for me to live here, since Jerry died. I just can't bear the idea of your stirring up more trouble."

"He didn't die. He was killed. And I'm not making trouble. I'm simply not dodging it."

"You think I don't know he was killed? You think I could ever forget it? I know what the old ladies say about me behind my back. And the stodgy wives at their bridge parties, who think they're so God damn respectable! They think their husbands are such solid citizens, but most of them are too stupid to know where their money comes from. My husband was killed, but I get no sympathy from them. I wasn't born here, you see, and I made my own living before I was married, so I'm a suspicious character. It hasn't been easy for me. Sometimes I thought I'd go crazy with nobody to talk to."

"You shouldn't have such a hard time finding someone to talk to."

"Men, you mean? They've come sniffing around. I

could have their men, if I thought they were worth having."

"Why don't you leave here, if you don't like it? There are other cities. Where did you come from?"

She didn't answer for a minute. She went to the bar and poured herself another shot of whisky. When she had drunk it, she said: "I've got a business to run here. I'm carrying on."

"You got rid of the hotel fast enough."

"I told you I had to. Anyway, that's no concern of yours."

"Where did the money go?"

Alcohol had refueled her fires. She said fiercely: "I'm not answerable to you."

"I understand I'm next in line for J.D.'s property."

"As long as I'm alive I have a perfectly free hand."

I got up and walked towards her across the room. "Now I know where we stand," I said. "What makes you certain you're going to be alive very long?"

With my shoulders coming towards her, it must have sounded like a direct threat. Her face went to pieces finally. She moved back into the corner between the bar and the wall, watching me with a basilisk grin, the breath hissing in her nostrils.

"Get away from me," she whispered.

I leaned on the bar and smiled as cheerfully as I could. "You scare easily, don't you? You've got a lot of fear inside you, but I didn't put it there. I'm just the peg you're hanging it on for the moment. Now I wonder where all that fear came from?"

Her whole face was twisting, trying to cover the nakedness of her emotion. "Go away," she whispered again. "I can't stand any more of your talk."

"I'm not crazy about it myself, but there isn't much else I can do. Now, if you'd do a little of the talking and tell me what you're afraid of—"

"You came here to torment me, didn't you?" she said in a low monotone. "You thought you could break me down. You hate me because your father left me his money, and you think you should have it. Get out of here, you overgrown bully!"

I was young enough to be hit hard by the epithet. But before I walked out of the house I threw her something to chew in bed:

"What you need is a good psychiatrist. I hear there's a good one in the state penitentiary."

Chapter 5

A faded sign in the window of Kaufman's second-hand store stated: "We Buy, Sell, and Exchange Anything," and the contents of the window supported the statement. There were old coats, cameras, military medals, an old fox neckpiece, which looked as if it had been gnawing itself to death, a Western saddle, a shotgun, a pair of Indian clubs, a rusty pair of handcuffs, a thirty-day clock in a bell jar, a complete set of the *Waverley* novels, a bird cage, a greasy truss. The strangest object in the window was a lithographed portrait of Friedrich Engels, surveying with a cold eye the chaotic symbols of the civilization he had criticized.

The store was dark, but a thin line of light shone under a door at the back. I knocked. The door at the back opened, and a bulky shadow appeared in the rectangle of light, walking not quite like a man. He switched on the store lights and hobbled towards me, through a junk heap of rusty stoves, baby carriages whose original occupants had long since graduated from high school, fly-specked dishes, and battered furniture—the detritus of broken homes and the leavings of people bettering themselves on the installment plan.

He was a heavy old man who swung one leg stiffly from the hip and rolled as he walked. He flattened his broad nose against the window in the front door and peered at me. Then he shouted through the pane: "What do you want? I'm all closed up."

I shouted back: "Are you the man that writes the letters to the newspapers?"

"I'm the man. You been reading them?"

"Let me in. I want to talk to you."

He unsnapped a key ring from his belt, unlocked

37

and opened the door. "So what do you want to talk to me about? Ideas?"

The smile which swallowed his eyes was wide, bland, and simple, like the smile on a Buddha's stone face. The naked crown of his head was level with my chin, but he was almost as wide as the door. He swung his stiff leg and moved back out of my way.

"What's Engels doing in the window?" I asked.

"You know his face? Almost nobody in this godforsaken burg knows him. They ask me who's that, is that your father? So I tell them who Engels was. I tell them what he stood for. I educate them without their knowing what I'm doing." He sighed heavily. "The exploited masses."

"A good many of the exploited masses must come in here. You're in a good spot to spread your gospel."

"You come in the back." Without touching me, his right arm moved in the circular gesture of embrace. "I like to talk to a man who knows ideas."

He led me down a narrow aisle to the back of the store, through a tiny office containing a high bookkeeper's desk, into his living apartment. The room where he invited me to sit down was a combination of living-room and kitchen. There were a deal table, a few old leather chairs and some painted wooden ones, a bookcase in one corner, a gas plate on the shelf beside the sink. Above the bookcase there was an amateurish pencil sketch of Karl Marx.

"Why don't you put Marx in the window?"

"Then not so many people would ask me who he was, because they know. I wouldn't have a chance to educate them."

"You've been in this town a long time, haven't you, Mr. Kaufman?"

"Nearly all my life. I've been right here in this location for the last thirty-five years."

"You should be able to tell me something about the municipal government. Where's the real power in the town?"

"You a reporter? Or writing a book?"

"I'm gathering material," I said.

He didn't ask me what kind of material. He smiled more blandly than before, and said: "You want it the way they spell it out in the papers for the exploited masses? Or do you want it the way I see it? Sometimes I think, especially since they threw out the labor organizers in the rubber factories—I think I'm the only man in town who isn't stone blind."

"Spell it out your way."

He leaned back in his wide chair and bent his good leg over his stiff one. "According to the city charter the city's laws are made by a city council of twelve members elected annually by the people, voting according to wards. The mayor, elected annually by the people at large, is the head of the executive branch of the city government, and he administers the city laws as passed by the council."

"Who runs the police?"

"A police board, of which the mayor is an ex-officio member. The other three members are appointed for overlapping periods of three years by the city council. All that is the way it's written down in the charter."

"And who actually runs the town?"

"Alonzo Sanford dominates the town. But you can't say he actually runs it. For a good many years he had a working alliance with a man called J.D. Weather. Weather got hold of a slot-machine concession for this area, and over a period of years he developed into an old-fashioned city boss. He spent money in the right places and got his hands on the council and the police force. At the same time he was pushing down roots, staging political picnics, helping the little people out of jams, getting them medical care when they couldn't pay for it, helping families to get on relief, contributing to campaigns run by the Poles and the Serbs and the Italians and the other minorities. It got so everybody in town knew him, and most of them liked him. They knew they could count on J.D. Weather in a pinch, and they voted the way he wanted them to. He never held any office himself, but the last fifteen years no mayor or councilman could get elected in this town unless he gave him the nod."

"Where does Alonzo Sanford come into this?"

"For one thing, because a man like Weather couldn't get away with corrupting the city government without help. The so-called better people would run him out of town. Sanford was his high-class protection."

"I don't see what Sanford got out of the deal."

"Everything he wanted," the old man said—"men in office who wouldn't tax his real estate too hard; police who would help to keep union activity out of his plants. And, working through J.D. Weather, he could stay in the background and pose as a grand old citizen. As long as they didn't touch him, the maggots could eat up the town."

It was painful to hear my father talked about like that. I had never lost the conception of him that I had formed as a boy: leading citizen, square businessman, straight talker, everybody's friend. "Was J.D. Weather that bad?"

"He was bad for the town. I don't think he ever took direct graft himself, but he made it possible for others to take it. Once corruption starts, it always spreads, right down to the policeman on his beat, taking a cut from a floozie or protecting a petty thief. Personally, J.D. Weather wasn't a bad man. He did a lot of good for individuals—that was one of his holds on the town. But he interfered with the democratic processes and corrupted this city from the top down—all so he could rake in a thousand a week from his slot machines, and feel generous and powerful into the bargain."

"You didn't like him much."

"Why is this town twenty years behind the times?" he snorted. "Underpaid men and women in the rubber plants, working for fifteen-twenty dollars a week. They try to do something for themselves, and the cops take their leaders to the edge of town and give them a beating and send them up the road. Slot machines and poolrooms and whorehouses, instead of playgrounds and community houses to keep the juvenile delinquents from going delinquent. Some of the worst slums in the country, with Alonzo Sanford taking in high rents from them. Why do things stay that way? Because they conspired to keep 'em that way. I thought things might start to be different when Allister got in year before last——"

"It's funny," I said. "I asked you about the town, and you give me past history. J.D. Weather's been dead for two years."

"But the melody lingers on, boy. That's what I can't understand about Allister."

"He's the mayor now, isn't he?"

"He's been mayor for nearly two years. He ran on a reform platform. He promised to clean up the town. He was a young lawyer out of the D.A.'s office, and he talked like a fighter, and I thought he meant it. So did a lot of other people; he got the support of the honest middle-class elements, and the workers that had any idea what was good for them. After J.D. Weather got killed, he practically swept the town. He knew the facts of municipal corruption, and he didn't pull any punches. That was during his campaign for election. But when he got in, things went on as before. Last year he came up for re-election, and he toned down his talk a lot. He didn't go in for facts any more, he went in for high-sounding generalities. But he got in by a whopping majority, because there wasn't any opposition worth talking about."

"How do you account for that? You'd expect Sanford to oppose him."

"I think Jefferson was right," the old man said gravely. "Power corrupts. Why should Sanford and the forces of reaction oppose a man if they can absorb him and use him? I don't know a darn thing about it, but I'm suspicious Sanford is grooming him to take J.D. Weather's place. All I know is this. Allister hasn't moved a muscle in nearly two years in the mayor's office. He rants about evil in the city, but he never seems to put his finger on any of it. He spends his time building up his political machine. I guess power corrupted him, or maybe Sanford's money hypnotized him. I don't know. Anyway, it's an example of the difficulty of reform by constitutional methods. I'm not a gradualist myself."

"I didn't expect you'd be." I glanced at the picture

of Marx on the wall. "But anything else is pretty precarious, isn't it? You're liable to lose what freedom you've got while you think you're fighting for more freedom."

"What freedom have they got?" he demanded. "Freedom to slave in the factories, vote and think the way the radio and newspapers and political bosses tell them to vote and think, freedom to befuddle their brains in the taverns and the moving picture shows: freedom to be exploited and dispossessed. Let them stand up and fight for their rights!"

"I was wondering," I said slowly, "I was wondering if J.D. Weather could have been shot by somebody who disapproved of him for political reasons."

"You're a cop!" He levered himself to his feet with a hoarse grunt. "I thought I knew all the dirty cops in the town, but you're a dirty cop I didn't know." His face was massive and calm, and he was breathing heavily through his nose.

"Were you accused of killing him at first?"

"I said my say long ago," he growled. "A dirty cop coming to me, pretending to be interested in ideas. You can get out."

I stayed in my chair. "What I've seen of the cops here, I don't like them any better than you do. I came to you for information."

"Who are you then?" His key ring clinked on his belt with the angry heaving of his belly.

"John Weather is my name. We were talking about my father."

He sat down heavily in his chair and blinked his innocent old eyes. "Why didn't you tell me? I wouldn't talk that way to a son about his father."

"I guess I didn't know my father very well," I said. "I was only twelve when I saw him last, and, even then, I spent most of my time away at school. But I wanted information, and I got it. There's some other information I want. The gun that killed him came out of your store."

For the first time a glaze of cautious insincerity came over his eyes. "That revolver was stolen from my store.

It was in the window, and somebody stole it from there."

I said: "You talk a good fight, Kaufman. You rant about cleaning up this city. But when you have a chance to help catch a murderer, you back down. I didn't think a man like you could be scared so badly."

"Scared, phooey!" he exploded. "Why should I talk to a Cossack like Hanson? He put me in the clink one time for addressing a meeting. He drove some of my best friends out of town."

"You've never seen me before tonight. You can talk now."

"What are you doing in this town?"

"I came here to look for a job, and I found one waiting for me—the job of finding out who killed my father."

"I can't tell you that, boy. If you think it was me, you don't know me. It's the system I want to see destroyed."

"You're helping to keep things the way they are by clamming up."

"Understand this, if I talked to you I'd be taking a chance. I'd be taking a chance on you. If you ran to the cops with your story, they'd have something on me, and they've been trying to get something on me all my life. I got too many ideas in my head. If you went to certain other people, maybe I wouldn't live very long."

"Maybe you won't live very long anyway. You're nearly seventy, aren't you?"

"Seventy-five," he said with a smile. "I'm old enough to take a chance."

"I'm twenty-two—young enough to make trouble. You might be able to help me make a lot of trouble."

"Joey Sault's about your age. He used to spend a lot of time in this store before my granddaughter left."

"Joey Sault?"

"He went to the reformatory for shoplifting when he was still a juvenile. I never thought he'd try it on me, though. He was going straight, and I thought Carla and him were going to get married."

"If this Joey Sault took the gun, why didn't you tell the police?"

"I already told you one reason. I don't trust the police, and I don't like them. There's another reason. Joey could have got a long term in the pen for larceny. Maybe for accessory to murder."

"Or murder."

"Maybe so. But I happen to know he didn't do it."

"You seem sure of yourself. How do you know?"

"He told me he didn't. I asked him."

"And you believed what he told you?"

"He's no good at lying," the old man said. "If he had been lying, I would have known. He stole the gun and sold it. He refused to tell me where he sold it. What could I do?" He spread his thick hands.

"So you held up a murder investigation because a small-time thief wanted to marry your granddaughter."

"You simplify too much," he said with weary patience. "I tried to save him from the consequences of his own actions. They were more serious consequences than he deserved, at least that's what I thought then. Anyway, he never married Carla. It turned out later all he wanted to do was ruin her and pimp for her. Maybe he's pimping for her now. I heard she's been out at the Cathay Club the last few months."

"I don't like the sound of Sault."

"Joey is a product of conditions," the old man said gravely. "His father was a cheap bookie, his mother left him young, the gangs in the south-side slums brought him up. His sister is a prosperous whore. Naturally he should want to be a pimp. What other use would he have for his good looks?"

"Where can I find this good-looking boy?"

"He used to live with his sister. Her name is Mrs. Sontag—Francesca Sontag. In the Harvey Apartments, on Sandhurst, three blocks south of Main."

I got up and said: "You're not taking a chance on me. I think some of your ideas are screwy, but you're the first honest man I've talked to here. I won't let you down."

He reached out and took hold of my arm. "Wait until you've lived seventy-five years and tell me what you think of my ideas. And be careful of Joey. He carries a knife."

"I have a feeling I'll probably live to be seventy-five," I said before he closed the door.

Chapter 6

The Harvey Apartments was one of the newer build-ings in the belt of apartments between the downtown business section and the south-side factory district. It couldn't have been built more than seven or eight years before, but already its stucco skin was beginning to crack and peel. Already its jerry-built pretentious-ness was warping and fading into harmony with the streets of dismal tenements that flanked it, like a mid-dle-class dream subsiding into lower-class reality. Peo-ple would live here, I thought, whose finances, or whose morals, barred them from the good residential districts. Still, it could seem like a lot of class to a slum-bred petty shoplifter.

Baby carriages gave the lower hallway a family air of struggling respectability. But many of the cards over the rusting mailboxes on the wall bore the names of married women living, it appeared, alone. Mrs. Sonia Weil. Mrs. Dorothy Williams. Mrs. Francie Sontag was among them. Her apartment number was 23, and I climbed to the second floor and found it. The mutter and growl of two voices behind the door, a man's and a woman's, ceased when I knocked.

But it was a full minute before the door was opened. Mrs. Sontag was in pink silk negligee which revealed and exaggerated the amplitude of her figure. Her heavy, black hair was down her back. Her bold, soft face might once have been very handsome, and might still have been amiable.

"What do you want?" she said in a brisk, forbidding voice, which implied that I was entitled to no wishes. Over her frilled shoulder I could see a dark-grey pin-striped coat laid across one arm of the red satin chesterfield. I couldn't be sure in the dim, aphrodisiac light of her rose-shaped lamps, but it looked like the coat of a man's suit.

"I'd like to speak to Mr. Joseph Sault. Your brother?"

"Joe isn't here." She made a move to shut the door in my face.

"Can't you tell me where I can find him?" I said quickly. "It's business I want to see him about."

"What kind of business?" Her bright black eyes looked into my face with caution. A movement of air in the apartment behind her flooded my nostrils with her perfume. It was good perfume.

From somewhere out of sight a man's voice called: "Who is it, Francie?"

"Somebody wants to see Joe."

"I'm in the market," I told her. "There's something I want to buy from him."

It made no sense to me, but it seemed to make sense to her. "He should be in back of the poolroom. You know, where they run the poker game."

I picked a name out of my memory of the neon signs on Main Street: "Weber's?"

"No, Charlie's." She closed the door so sharply it cut my "Thank you" in half.

She went back to her strenuous profession, and I went back to the street. My drive was a long way from running down, but I was beginning to feel just a little like a salesman of something nobody wanted. Or a billiard ball looking for a carom and finding nothing to hit.

But I still felt like a special kind of billiard ball, not subject to the forces of gravity and friction. I walked the three blocks to the corner of Main Street in three minutes. Without seeming to go anywhere, the night crowds were thinning out, as if there were trap doors in the pavement. But there was a higher proportion of drunks, and fewer unassorted couples. The bars were beginning to empty, and the night-blooming floozies were steering their catches to the walk-up apartments and sleazy hotels they called home.

There was a tall, blue policeman on the corner, watching the crowds benevolently like a pagan god at a carnival in his honor. He was very tall and very fat, looking the way a cop should look if he isn't expected to catch anything.

I planted myself in front of him, and after a minute he looked down at me with a pained expression on his serene stultified face. "Anything I can do for you?"

"Can you tell me where Charlie's poolroom is?"

"Ain't it a little late for playing pool?" He winked with an effort that twisted the corner of his mouth.

"What time does it close—at twelve? There should be time for one game."

I had amused him. He laughed and slapped the holster on his hip. "Sure, there is. But watch yourself, kid. You don't look any too well heeled. The stakes are pretty high in Charlie's game."

"Where is it?" I said sharply.

"All right, don't get peppery. I was just going to tell you." He pivoted on his base and pointed down West Main Street. "Two blocks down to your left. I warned you, don't forget."

"Why should I struggle for a second million?" I asked him over my shoulder, and left him winking both eyes.

Charlie's Billiard Emporium and Soft Drinks was a little tobacco shop with a big basement underneath. The shirt-sleeved man behind the counter gave me a sleepy look, snapped one of his purple arm bands like a signal to himself, and went back to his racing sheet. I went down the unswept stairs and stood at the foot for a moment, peering through the smoke-blue air. The smoke haze hung in the wide, low room like a cloudy liquid, through which men appeared like half-human creatures moving slowly over a sea floor in an undersea ritual. The click of billiard balls cracked the illusion, and I went on into the room.

The walls were partly lined with cue racks, some of which were padlocked. There must be players here who took the game seriously, to own their own cues. Between the racks were group portraits of old football teams, some with handlebar mustaches; signed photos of game little forgotten fighters, with huge fists and shoulders leaning gamely into the camera and tiny disappearing waists; an unknown wrestler, wearing a championship belt almost as wide as a corset, who signed himself: "All the Best to My Old Pal Charlie, Al"; pictures of naked women as bright and empty as balloons; advertisements for rubber goods and specifics and quack doctors waiting for despair, when everything else had failed, to gravitate to them.

These Herculaneum murals depressed me, and I looked away into the room. There were six or eight tables, bright green under their double cones of light: a couple for snooker or English billards, one without pockets for three-cushion, the rest for ordinary pool. Most of the tables were being used by boys and young men who leaned over them in precise and prayerful attitudes or stood back in meditation chalking their cues. The cues shot forward quickly and certainly, like little goads of fate: the balls rearranged themselves according to the laws of physics, like well-trained molecules taken in infinitely slow motion, or infinitely miniature planets. Once a player miscued, and his ball jumped the table and rolled away on the floor among the filth of years.

A young man knocking the balls around at a table by himself scooped it up and tossed it back. He had white hair and a goose-flesh face as white as typewriter paper. The outer corners of his pale-pink eyes drooped towards the corners of his mouth, as if his face had been parted in the middle and combed backwards.

He went back to his game, shooting casually, and sank four balls in succession. I found a straight cue in one of the open racks, and asked him for a game.

"Plain pool, one-two-three?"

"Suits me," I said.

"For two bits?"

"I can use two bits."

He smiled sadly, set up the balls, won the flip, and broke them. I sank the one in a side pocket and nudged the two halfway down the cushion into the end. The three was behind a cluster of other balls, and I couldn't quite see it. I tried a cushion shot and hit the three but missed the side pocket by an inch. He couldn't see the three either, because the seven was in his way, but he put a lot of english on the right side of his ball and curved it around the seven. The three dropped in, and he'd left himself a setup for the four in the end pocket.

"Nice position," I said. "Seen anything of Joey tonight?"

"He was sitting in the back room until about an hour ago." He sank the four, drawing the cue ball into position for the five. Then he sank the five.

The six ball was an impossible shot, tight on the cushion at the other end of the table. He made it.

"Where is he now?"

His pale gaze stroked me mildly and returned to the table. He dropped the seven in the side pocket and left himself a setup for the eight. "You a friend of Sault's?"

I thought the business approach would be safest. "I'd like to be. I'm interested in buying what he's got to sell."

He sank the eight ball. "He wouldn't be doing any business tonight. He told me he's running a party for some of the girls."

"My business can't wait," I said. "Where is the party?"

The nine was in a tight spot, out of line with any of the pockets. He looked at it carefully, and the cue slid forward between his white fingers. The nine traveled the length of the table and rebounded into a side pocket.

"Where did you say the party was?"

"I didn't say. It's over at Garland's, beside the park."

He missed the ten. "Know where that is?"

"No. Do you?" I sank the ten and missed the eleven.

He took the eleven. "Opposite the main entrance of the park. On the top floor, up above the liquor store. If you do any business, tell him Whitey sent you."

He missed the twelve. I sank the twelve and then the rest of the balls. He grunted audibly when the fifteen went in.

"That was game ball," I said. "Tough luck."

He looked at me sadly. "I can put the game on the slate, but I ain't got your two bits. I got cleaned out in the back room. I didn't think you'd win."

"Forget it," I went away and left him knocking the balls around by himself.

My taxi dropped me in front of the closed iron gates of a municipal park. The night air was beginning to turn chilly, and the dark lawns beyond the gates, shaded by unbudding trees, were as desolate as any cemetery. In the center of the paved triangle of which the gates formed the base, there was a statue I remembered, an early French explorer in bronze buckskins.

"Meeting somebody?" the driver asked as I paid him off.

"Got an appointment with this statue. We get together every now and then to talk over old times."

He looked at me vacuously and I didn't tip him. When he had gone away I turned and looked at the statue. The statue didn't say anything. He stood calmly gazing with blind, metal eyes across a virgin country that no longer existed. I remembered from school that he had left France with the intention of bringing Christianity to the heathen.

On the opposite corner there was a palsied neon sign: "Liquor Store." Above it were three stories of flats. Five or six of the windows on the top floor were lighted, but all the blinds were drawn. They weren't drawn tight enough to contain the shouts and laughter which I heard. It was high, wild laughter, definitely not merry, but I didn't mind. Merry laughter would have conflicted with my mood.

I crossed the street and found the entrance to the flats beside the store front. The narrow stairs were lit, or unlit, by red twenty-watt bulbs, one to each flight. The bulb at the top of the fourth flight was white but grimy. It cast a bad light on a sky-blue door trimmed with red by an amateurish hand. The same hand had painted "F. Garland" on the door in tall, red letters which bled a little.

The sounds of the party came through the thin panels like water through a sieve. I had listened to a lot of parties, and I knew that mixed parties sound like a monkeyhouse, female parties like an aviary, and stag parties like a kennel. This party sounded like a kennel, though some of the voices were lap-dog voices, high and querulous.

I knocked on F. Garland's door, wondering where the girls were. The yapping and whining and howling and barking went right on. A fire-siren laugh climbed little steps all the way up to a high, idiot cackle, and teetered shakily down. I knocked again.

A small man came to the door and opened it, still buttoning up his clothes. The smudge of lipstick on his narrow chin was the only spot of color in his face. It was a pathetic little face, with hollow cheeks, high, thin temples, a young, sensitive mouth, whose upper lip overlapped the lower lip a trifle. His voice was soft and pleasant:

"I don't think I know you, do I?"

"The loss is mine. Is Joe Sault here?"

"Joey is occupied at present." He uttered a shameful, little, lilting laugh. His gray eyes were as amiable as ground glass.

"Will you tell him I'd like to see him for a minute? Out here will do."

"Is it business?"

"Call it that."

"He's not doing business yet tonight. He's waiting for more stock."

"Not that kind of business. I have to talk to him."

"What name shall I give him, fellow?"

"John Weather. You his secretary?"

An angry flush pumped a little color into his phthisical cheeks. He sneered at me with his expressive nostrils. "My name is Garland," he said softly. "Maybe you'd better remember that."

"Delighted, I'm sure. Convey my respects to Mr. Sault, and tell him I await his pleasure in the antechamber."

"A gagman," he chirped. He shut the door, but before it closed I saw the scrambled bodies inside the room. They were live bodies, but I had experienced stronger fellow feeling with corpses.

A minute later the handsome boy came to the door. He had sideburns, dimples, swimming black eyes. He had chocolate-brown high-rise trousers with three pleats on each side, and scarlet silk suspenders to hold them up under his armpits. His shirt was made of beige silk. He had the rank masculinity of a tomcat, but his dark face was emotionally versatile. The cigarette between his slender brown fingers burned unevenly and did not smell like tobacco.

"Joe Sault?"

"You've got me." He smiled engagingly. "Garland doesn't like you."

"I like Garland ever so much."

"He's screwy, but he's got a good nose. When he don't like 'em, I often don't like 'em."

"And here I was thinking my personality was irresistible. You're destroying my dream."

"You talk too much, like Garland says." His expression shifted easily from boyish friendliness to blank hostility. "If you got something to say to me, say it." His cigarette had burnt down to his fingers. He ground it out on the doorjamb and put the butt in his pocket.

I drew back on my right foot and shifted my weight to a position of equilibrium, ready to move in any direction. "I need a gun," I said.

He slid past me on quiet feet and leaned over the shaky banister to peer down the stairs to the next landing. "Why come to me?" he asked me over his shoulder. "They got guns for sale in stores."

"I'm hot. A couple of years ago—" I paused, waiting for his mind to add one and one.

He straightened up and faced me. He was almost as tall as I was, and his shoulders were very good. I readjusted my weight in relation to his new position.

He said in a tone of gentle reminiscence: "You were saying: 'A couple of years ago.' "

"You helped out a friend of mine."

"Who is this friend of yours?" He stood back and watched my face impassively, with both hands in his pockets.

"He wouldn't want his name used. You know that."

"How did I help this friend of yours a couple of years ago that wouldn't want his name used?"

"Don't you remember?"

"I helped a lot of people. I'm a very helpful guy."

"You got him a Smith and Wesson revolver—"

The muscles moved in his right arm, all the way up to the shoulder and across to the pectoral. He said very quietly: "What did you say your name was?"

"Your memory is bad." I was as tense as he was. "John Weather."

The knife flew open as it came out of the pocket. My left hand was ready and caught his right wrist. My right arm put a lock on it. He twisted quickly and pulled hard, but not out of my grasp. He was hard to bend, but he bent slowly as I raised my hands locked over his wrist. Slowly his head went down. He sighed almost inaudibly and the knife fell free just before I tore his shoulder loose in its socket.

Suddenly I let go, stepped in close to him, and brought my right fist up from the knee. The point of his chin bruised my knuckles, his head went back and rapped on the wall. For a moment he stood there on weak knees, both hands outspread flat against the wall, his head sagging. A voice from the doorway stopped my left in the middle of the concluding punch:

"Don't hit Joey again. It could spoil our party if you did."

Garland stepped through the door and closed it behind him. His sensitive little mouth was quivering, but his right hand was in his coat pocket holding something solid and steady.

I took a step backwards so that I could watch both of them, and in the same movement I stooped and had the knife. "I'll keep this. I make a collection of knives that try to cut me." I pressed the catch and forced the four-inch blade back to its place in the handle, then dropped it my pocket.

"You want me to call some of the fellows, Joey?" Garland said.

Sault was smoothing his hair, rubbing his jaw, massaging his dented personality. "We handle this hard boy ourselves. Tell him to give me back my knife."

"Give him back his knife."

"I wouldn't want him to cut himself."

He jerked his heavy pocket. "Give it back."

"It's for my collection," I said. "My friend who sent me here wouldn't like it if you shot me. And most wounds would give me time to throw you downstairs."

"He thinks I couldn't give him a head wound from the hip," Garland said to Sault. He giggled like a mischievous little girl. "Tell him about me, Joey."

"He's fast," Joey said sullenly. "And his name's Weather, he says. We wouldn't want to kill him here and spoil the party, like you said."

"Sault doesn't sound gay," I said to Garland. I was getting tired of watching both of them, shifting my weight with every heartbeat. "Maybe what he needs is for you to get him another reefer."

"Say the word, Joey. It would be nice to shoot him."

Sault's face was working with thought. Finally he said: "Lay off him, Garland. Maybe we better take it to Kerch."

"Who is Kerch?" I said.

"You don't want to know," Sault said. "You may think you do, but you don't want to know."

"Kerch is the man I work for," Garland said. "I work for Kerch twenty-four hours a day."

"You better take some of your overtime and buy yourself something to eat. You look hungry."

"I look better than dead people look."

"Take a look in your mirror. You'll be surprised."

"You go away from here," Garland said in a thin menacing voice. "But quick."

"Natch, Gloria. Natch."

I went down the stairs, not too fast and not too slow, feeling five eyes on my back: Sault's black eyes, Garland's gray eyes, and the hidden eye of the gun.

Chapter 7

There was nothing Oriental about the Cathay Club except its name and an insane plaster turret, of remotely Byzantine influence, over the front entrance. It was a long, white two-storied building, standing by itself a hundred feet back from the highway on the west side of town. It was just outside the city limits, and the taxi driver charged me two dollars to take me there.

It cost me another dollar to get in, since a fat man in a decaying tuxedo collected the cover charge at the door. I had seen the place before, but I had never been inside. It was like a hundred other city-limit night clubs all over the country—a room as big and as roughly built as a barn, the cheap simplicity of its construction concealed by dim lighting and fire-hazard decorations. A tiered orchestra stand at the back, precariously supporting an apathetic and underpaid Negro orchestra. In front of the orchestra stand, a dance floor, where the crowds of paying customers walked around in time to the music, and the paid entertainers sweated out their three-a-day. The rest of the floor was packed elbow to elbow and back to back with rickety little tables and uncomfortable little chairs. A blonde waitress in a bright red slack suit led me to one of them, and brought me a ninety-cent drink as hard to swallow as an insult.

"You missed Archie Calamus," she said. "He's the best number in the floor show. Where he takes off the young girl getting ready to go to a party—"

"I'd certainly hate to miss Archie," I told her.

"He comes on again at 3 A.M., if you want to wait. This is only the second show."

"That's swell," I said, thinking how disappointed

she'd be when she didn't get the tip she was working
for.

A Hawaiian dancer with Polish blue eyes from the
northwest side of Chicago came on the floor and rotated her hips, which looked fine for child-bearing. She
did a few concluding bumps, with percussion accom-
paniment by the orchestra, and swaggered massively
off. The crowd clapped.

"And now, ladies and gentlemen," said the slender,
dark young man who served as master of ceremonies,
"I take great pride and pleasure in presenting to you a
fine young singer whom you all know. That sensational
lyric tenor, Ronald Swift."

The crowd clapped and laughed. "You tell 'em,
Ronnie," a woman yelled.

The dark young man stayed where he was at the microphone and began to sing in a limply endearing way.
I looked around at the audience. It seemed prosperous
and indiscriminate. Young couples waiting for their
chance to dance, and above all to take or be taken
home. Older couples from the stores and insurance
companies and factory offices nibbling with a delightful
sense of shame and daring at their bimonthly slice of
life. Middle-aged men paternally fondling their young
companions. Some middle-aging women striving a little
desperately with smiles and chatter to hold the attention
of their younger escorts. A few unattached girls and
women drinking alone, their eyes on the prowl. All but
the last were drunk enough to be enjoying themselves.

The sensational lyric tenor became a master of ceremonies again, and announced a sensational Spanish
dance team. The man was drying up with age, and the
woman was getting too heavy, but they danced well.
The dialogue of their castanets was as sharp as good re-
partee. When their intricate steps brought them together, passion crackled between them like electricity.
Their stamping was as violent and real as love or hate.
They left the floor with wet faces, walking stately together.

Somebody close behind me was saying: "I didn't

think Kerch'd be able to keep his slot-machine racket after Allister got in."

"He had a lot of you bastards fooled," a brash salesman's voice cut in. "I could've told you what'd happen, and it happened."

"You mean nothing happened."

"Absolutely. What'd you expect to happen? It's always the same when these wild-eyed reformers get in. I seen it happen when I was a kid in Cleveland. But what the hell are you kickin' about?"

"Who's kickin'! I always said a wide-open town was good for business. Which is why I didn't come out for Allister."

"You might as well next time. Looks as if he's going to be with us a long time."

The orchestra began to play dance music. "C'mon, Bert," a woman whined. "We didn't come here to talk politics. Let's dance before it gets too crowded."

"Absolutely, Marge. Absolutely."

I saw them step onto the dance floor, a florid man in Harris tweeds, with his thick arm around the waist of a fading blonde.

"He knows his way around," the other man said behind me. "Bert's a good head."

"He's too fat," a woman said. "You're not too fat."

One of the unattached girls sat down opposite me at my table. Her thick brown hair swung forward and brushed her white shoulders. Her face was solemn and young, with steady somber eyes and a still mouth too garishly painted.

"A nice boy like you," she recited, "shouldn't be sitting all by his lonesome."

"A nice girl like you shouldn't be wasting her time on a guy like me."

"Why, what's the matter with you? I think you're kind of cute."

"You flatter me."

"Sure. Now that I've flattered you, you can buy me a drink."

I said: "The approach abrupt. Do I look well heeled?"

"Appearances are so deceptive."

"In your case, for example. You've got your face made up to suit this joint. Protective coloration, they call it in biology."

"Kid me some more," she said flatly. "You can if you buy me a drink. Biology is a very interesting subject."

"I like my biology experimental. Not cut and dried."

"You're not flattering me. I'll go away unless you buy me a drink."

"And take all the beauty out of my life? Just when my heart was opening up like a flower?"

"To hell with you!" she said suddenly and fiercely. She stood up and flung back her hair. Her slender body looked a little incongruous in a low-cut gown.

"Sit down again," I said. "What are you drinking?"

She sat down again. "Scarlett O'Hara."

"Are you on the staff of this enterprise?"

"Now, what would make you think that?" she said bitterly. "I come out here every night because I like it."

"You should be studying biology in school."

"I tried that. It didn't pay well. They expected to get it for free."

The waitress came over, and I ordered our drinks.

"Well," the girl said. "You certainly made me work for it."

"I'm not as well heeled as my appearance deceived you into not thinking I was."

"How you twist the language. You remind me of my grandfather."

"I'm not really that old. It's just the hard life I've led."

She raised her thin eyebrows. Her eyes were soft and young, but there was a hard glaze over them. "Quite a line you've got. I never saw you here before, did I?"

"Never been here before. Think of what I've been missing."

"What's your name?"

"John. What's yours?"

"Carla." So this was Kaufman's granddaughter.

"What's the name of your boss?"

"Kerch. Mr. Kerch is *so* lovely to work for."

"Everywhere I go," I said, "people tell me the most wonderful things about Mr. Kerch."

"You must run in some awful peculiar circles."

"I do—and Mr. Kerch is always at the center of them."

"You're kidding me again."

"I never kid when I'm talking about Mr. Kerch."

"You sound as if you don't like him."

"Do you?"

She leaned forward with her elbows on the table, her pointed chin supported on her palms. Her arms were round and slender, covered with a light golden fuzz, which caught the light like a faint phosphorescence. "It turns my stomach when he looks at me," she said. "When he touches me, I want to go home and take a bath."

"Does he go in for touching you a good deal?"

She lengthened her mouth at the corners in an expression of dull irony. "More or less."

"Why don't you go home and take a bath and stay home?"

"Who'd pay the water bill? And who the hell do you think you are, an evangelist or something?"

"I just don't like to see people playing themselves for a sucker."

Our drinks came, and the girl raised her pink cocktail: "Here's to you, sucker."

"Hello, sucker." My second drink tasted better than my first one.

"How well do you know Kerch?" she said after a pause.

"Don't know him at all."

"That's funny. You were talking as if you knew him."

"I don't have to know him not to like him, if that's what you mean."

"Wait till you get to know him. Then you'll really not like him."

"I wish he'd try to touch me. I'd tear him down and rebuild him."

"Don't try that," she said soberly. "You'd get hurt."

"Don't tell me he's a tough boy in addition to all his other virtues."

"He's not tough." There was a contemptuous snarl in her taut voice. "He's as soft as jelly—but he's got tough boys working for him."

"Like Garland? He'd make some man a good wife."

"You know Garland, do you? It's true what I said, appearances are deceptive. Garland is a very dangerous boy."

"He wouldn't be so dangerous if somebody took his gun away."

"Maybe not. But who's going to take his gun away? It's been tried."

"So what happened?"

"So there was business for the morgue. Kerch has Jahnke, too. Rusty makes the slot-machine collections. He hasn't got much on the ball, but he's pretty rugged. He used to be a boxer when he was in Pittsburgh."

She finished her drink and held up the empty glass. "All this talking makes me thirsty."

"I'll get you a glass of water."

She laughed. "You're the damndest cheapskate I ever sat down with."

"How much of a cut do you get on a drink?"

"Couldn't we keep this on a glamorous basis?"

"How glamorous? Champagne?"

She laughed again. "Thirty cents. Thirty cents a drink. Just like piecework in the rubber factory."

"Except that this is cleaner work, I suppose?"

"In a way, it is. In case you're wondering, I tried working in the rubber factory. It wasn't for me. I didn't like the smell. I didn't like what it did to my hands. And I don't like getting pushed around."

"You have pretty hands."

"Think so?" she said without enthusiasm. "It's about time you flattered me a little. You make a girl feel she's losing her grip."

I caught the waitress's eye and ordered two more drinks.

"You say you don't like being pushed around, but you work here. Don't you get pushed around quite a bit?"

"Yeah," she said. "That's why I'm getting out of here. As soon as I can save a little money, I'm shaking the dirt of this town off my feet."

"Where are you going?"

"I don't care where I go, as long as it's a long way from here. Maybe Chicago."

"What would you do there?"

"I got a friend in Chicago. You're kind of a nosy parker, aren't you?"

"Not all the time. I like you."

She gave me a long, straight look. For a moment her mouth and eyes forgot to be hard.

"I like anybody who doesn't like Kerch," I went on.

"Oh," she said.

"What does Kerch look like?"

"Why should you be so interested in him if you don't know him?"

"He did me a bad turn once."

"What kind of a bad turn?"

"The kind I don't talk about. What does he look like?"

"He's probably in the back office now. Why don't you go and take a look for yourself?"

"Maybe I will," I said. "But I like to know what I'm looking for."

"Did you ever read the fairy story about the frog king? My mother used to read it to me when I was a kid. Anyway, it's about a man that got changed by magic into a frog, and then changed back into a man. That's the way Kerch looks, as if he didn't change all the way back into a man."

"I wonder why Mrs. Weather would pick a guy like that to run her night club."

"Ask me another. He's smart, though. He's too goddam smart. But I don't think that's the reason he's working for her."

"Why, then?"

"If you ask me, he's not working for her, he's working for himself."

"She owns this place, doesn't she?"

"She's supposed to. But I've seen her out here talking to him a few times. He doesn't take his orders from her."

"Did he buy it from her?"

"I wouldn't know. I never heard that he did. The way she looks at him, I wouldn't be surprised if he had something on her."

"Such as?"

"What is this, the third degree? You ask more questions than a quiz program."

"Maybe that's the sixty-four-dollar question," I said.

"I was just telling you how it looked to me. I don't know of any special reason for her to be afraid of Kerch. Everybody's a little bit afraid of him."

"Are you?"

"No," she said slowly, "I don't think I am. I hate his guts too much to be afraid of him."

"Why? Has he got something on you?"

"The hell he has! I've got something on him. He likes doing some strange things." She was silent for a moment. "Why did you ask me if I was afraid of him? What difference does it make?"

I said in a low voice: "Because I'm going to get Kerch, and I can probably use some help."

"You a cop?"

"Not me. That's one reason I need help."

"You're biting off a big chunk of trouble if you think you're going to get Kerch. I told you he was smart, and I told you he's got tough boys working for him."

"I'm working for myself," I said, "so I put everything I've got into my work."

"I don't see how I could help you. If you're on the up-and-up, you better go and see Allister."

The florid man and his fading blonde had returned

to the table behind me. I noticed a pause in their conversation at the word "Allister."

"This isn't a good place to talk," I said. "Is there some place more private around here?"

"You can take me upstairs," she said demurely.

Chapter 8

The room to which she took me was furnished with a couple of cloth-covered chairs, a Hollywood bed with a bright silk cover, a dressing-table lit by a silk-shaded floor lamp, a washbasin in a corner behind a cheap Japanese screen. The single window was hung with a heavy drape, which seemed to cut the room off from time and space. But the sound of arriving and departing motors in the parking lot below the window sifted through the cloth like a muffled obbligato of impermanence.

She snapped the Yale lock and said uncertainly from the door: "You might as well sit down."

I took one of the chairs, and she sat facing me on the stool in front of the dressing-table.

"I didn't expect to be told to go to Allister," I said. "I thought he was protecting Kerch."

"Not Allister. He'd like to see him run out of town."

"What's he waiting for, then?"

"Allister isn't a fighter the way you are—at least, the way I think you are. His hands are tied, he says."

"Is he honest?"

"I think so," she said after a pause. "Anyway, I know he's Kerch's enemy."

"What makes you so sure?"

"I know him. He's a good friend of a friend of mine."

"I'll go and see what kind of a guy he is."

"He's clever. And he knows a lot about this town. He investigated it for the Cranbridge D.A., but they killed his report."

"Who killed it?"

66

"I heard it was a man called Weather. You wouldn't know him. He used to own this place."

"Oh."

She turned to the mirror, picked up a brush, and began to brush her hair with quick determined strokes. It flowed sleekly around the back of her head and billowed across her shoulders in soft copper gleaming curls. Embarrassment and a deeper feeling that masqueraded as pity made me feel restless and chilly. The brush swished and crackled through her hair like a tiger moving in the undergrowth.

"You don't live here, do you?" I said.

"God, no! I'd go crazy if I had to. I've got an apartment of my own."

"Where?"

Her eyes met mine in the mirror. The hair drawn smoothly back from her brow made her forehead look very young and pure. "Don't tell me you want to see me again?"

"I don't like the atmosphere here."

"Do I, though!"

"I'd like to come and see you where you live."

"I'm usually home in the afternoon. I live in the Harvey Apartments, they're south of Main—"

"I know where they are."

"I thought you didn't know this town?" She began to apply lipstick with a red-tipped little finger, stretching her mouth like a mask.

"I went there tonight to see a Mrs. Sontag."

"How do you happen to know her? Francie's a friend of mine."

"I don't. I was looking for her brother."

She whirled on her stool. "You bastard. You are a cop."

"Your family is allergic to cops, isn't it? Your grandfather had practically the same reaction."

Her small breasts rose and fell visibly with her quick breathing, and her hands were working at her sides. "You can get the hell out of here. And you can forget what I told you about where I live."

"So many people are taking me for a cop, I'm beginning to feel insulted."

"How do you know so much about me, then? Why did you come out here to find me?"

"But you found me. That was a coincidence. And I don't know a damn thing about you."

"You said you were talking to Grandfather."

"Not about you. He just happened to mention you."

"Who are you? What are you trying to do?"

"My father was this man Weather you said I wouldn't know. I'm trying to find out who killed him."

She watched my face in silence. Finally she said: "And you think it was Kerch?"

"My mind is open. What do you think?"

"I don't know anything about it. That was a long time before I came out here." After a moment she said shyly: "What did Grandfather say about me?"

I had to look for words. "He sounded kind of disappointed in you."

"The old fool!" she said bitterly. "I suppose he expects me to spend my life making his meals and cleaning up that dump of his and listening to his crazy lectures. He's screwy."

"Now I know what you meant when you said I reminded you of your grandfather."

A smile moved almost imperceptibly from her eyes to her mouth, but didn't stay. "No. I just meant you both like shooting off your mouths. He's all right, I guess. I feel sorry for him sometimes. He wanted me to get an education and be something. He's pretty well educated himself."

"Why did you leave him?"

"He ordered me out. He caught me with a boy in the back room." She was still for a time. Her eyes were looking at me, but they were blind and grim, turned inward on her young past. "I was just as glad, because I didn't want to stay anyway. He's a pretty good old man, but he didn't understand me at all. He had big ideas about helping people, but he never helped me. He thought I should go to normal school and be a teacher, can you imagine? He thought I was a crazy little bitch because I hated school. And then he was always writing radical letters to the newspapers, and the kids would come to school and take it out on me. I couldn't ever tell him about that, even."

"What happened to your mother and father?"

"I never saw my father. My mother died when I was eleven. After that Grandfather took care of me. He was nice to me when I was a kid. We used to go on picnics in the country."

"You never saw your father?"

She moved awkwardly and clasped her hands in her lap. "I was a bastard," she said violently. Then more softly: "I guess you think I'm taking after my mother."

"I'm not thinking a thing," I said. "Except that I've got another reason for not liking Sault."

She looked at me suspiciously. "You said my grandfather didn't talk about me."

"All he said was that he thought Sault was going to marry you, and he was wrong."

"How wrong he was! Isn't it a scream?" She spoke with strained vivacity. "That I should fall for the pretty eyes of a dirty thug like that. Wouldn't it've been swell to set up light housekeeping with that heel, so he could go the rounds of the poolrooms and drum up trade for me, and pay me off himself with a quick one every day? It makes me laugh every time I think of it."

"I don't see you laughing."

"No? for a long time I couldn't think of that crawling bastard without laughing. Now he means so little to me I can't even get a laugh out of him."

"He means enough to you to make you get all wound up."

"Hell, I'm wildly crazy about him! Didn't I make myself clear? I'd like to play marbles with those beautiful black eyes."

"He works for Kerch, doesn't he?"

"He did for a while. But even Kerch doesn't trust him. He milked some of the machines. I hear he's in business for himself now, peddling marijuana. It's a business that's just about low enough to suit him."

"He used to do some shoplifting," I said.

"Yeah, he got sent up for it. That's where he learned most of his little tricks—in reform school."

"With that record, I don't suppose your grandfather wanted him around the store?"

"Grandpa's a sucker for anybody that he thinks has missed the breaks. He kept an eye on Joey, but he didn't try to keep him out of the store."

"Did Sault ever steal anything from him?"

"No, not that I knew of. That's a funny thing, isn't it? When he started going with me, he said he was going straight. He did seem to be going straight, too. Christ, he even had me fooled!"

"Maybe he had himself fooled for a while."

She laughed shortly. "Not Joe Sault."

"But he never lifted anything from the store?"

"No, I guess there wasn't anything there he wanted. Except me."

"You make me mad," I said. "You look like a nice girl, and you talk like an honest one. But once upon a time you let a dimwit with sideburns take advantage of you. You woke up from love's young dream with a hangover. It could happen to anybody. It happens to more girls than you think. But what did you do? You sat back on your little tail and told yourself your life was finished—you were ruined for keeps. You knew damn well you were a romantic sap, so you set out to prove the opposite. You'd been too soft, so now you'd be too hard. You'd been tumbled once, so now you'd get yourself tumbled ten or twelve times a night. All to show yourself, and your dimwit with the sideburns, that you're a hard girl and can take it."

"You understand me so well," she said ironically. "You should put all that savvy to work and get yourself a job psychoanalyzing people or whatever they call it."

"I don't think you're so hard. I think I could push my finger right through your crust."

"You're the one that talks like a romantic softie. I suppose you read somewhere that a woman never forgets the first man she has. I wouldn't cross the street to spit on Sault if he was lying in the gutter, and one of these days he probably will be."

"That's not what I meant."

"I don't think you know what you meant," she said fiercely. "I suppose you think I give a damn for the men I bring up here. They don't mean any more to me than if they were made of wood. They can work and sweat on me, and they can't do anything to me. I can lie under a man and think about what I'm going to have for dinner tomorrow."

"It's a tough way to buy your dinners."

"Tough? It's soft and easy. It buys me the things I want. You think I care about myself? I don't. I admit I cared about myself the first time. After that it didn't matter. I don't care about myself at all. Nobody can do anything to me."

The hysterical rush of her words made a shrill babbling in the room. Her white hands wrestled each other in her lap.

"You talk like a hard little bitch," I said. "But you're a worried girl, and you don't like yourself very much."

"I like myself fine," she cried defiantly. "I like myself better than I like any soft-soaping preacher who goes around sticking his nose in other people's business." The stream of words ceased abruptly, as if a valve had been closed somewhere out of sight.

Suddenly she spread her hands over her face, ran blindly across the narrow room, and fell full length on the bed. The dry sobs that struggled up out of her chest shook her whole body. The bed creaked under her in facetious imitation of itself.

I got out of my chair and stood over her. She was lying face down across the bed, her head concealed under her scattered sheaf of hair. She was crying almost without sound now, but her body trembled convulsively. Little shivers of anguish moved rhythmically across her pale back, and her thin shoulder blades were tremulous. I felt I should cover her with something and leave her, but pity held me where I was. I was sorrier for her than I had ever been for anyone before.

Suddenly, as if a pressure had been removed from my groin, the pity turned into an overpowering hunger. I leaned across her and lifted her hair and kissed the nape of her neck. My hands burrowed under her body and found her sharp small breasts. I forgot the ugly room, the strangeness of the meeting, the dark past, and the dim future. So did she.

Her mouth was sweet. Her body was thin and desperate and sweet.

"Lie heavy on me. Hold me tight. Tighter."

"I wouldn't want to hurt you, lover."

"You couldn't hurt me."

The streams of our desire rose, met, mingled, and subsided. I felt empty, dazed, and spent. She was very gentle with me. We lay silent and still for a while, holding each other close.

"This is the queerest thing that ever happened to me," she said.

"To me, too."

"And the nicest."

She stood up smiling and went behind the screen in the corner. Her voice came above the intimate rustle of water running in the basin:

"I hope you don't think I brought you up here to—to seduce you."

"I think maybe you did at first. But you got over the idea. I did any seducing that was done."

"Isn't it crazy? I was bawling like a baby, and then it happened. But it seemed so natural."

"It's natural."

"But it happened so quick. I didn't know anything like that could come so quick."

"Anything like what?"

She came out from behind the screen, her face washed and shining, looking five years younger. She leaned over me and kissed me lightly. "I think you're nice."

"I'm not nice. But you are if you'll let yourself be."

She laughed in my face. "You look ridiculous. You've got lipstick all over you."

"I wonder where it came from."

"You know damn well where it came from." She kissed me again. "Go and wash your face."

When I had washed myself she was sitting in front of the dressing-table, brushing her hair again. The lucite brush flashed back and down, her curls rustling and blossoming under it.

"Don't do that," I said. "I can't stand seeing you brush your hair. It makes me feel funny."

"You'll just have to feel funny, then. I've got to go downstairs."

There were footsteps in the hall, and someone tried the door. Until then we might have been in a mountain cabin miles from anywhere, a stateroom on a ship at sea, a cell in the bowels of the earth. The meaning of the room returned like a bad taste in my mouth.

"Who is it?" she said, her eyes intent on her face in the mirror.

"Mabel. Is that you, Carla?"

"Just wait a minute, hon. I'll be out right away."

The voices of a man and a girl, talking and laughing, came through the door.

"I guess we've been in here a terribly long time." She closed her lips on a piece of Kleenex and stood up, straightening the shoulder straps of her gown. Armored in powder and paint, her face had reverted to its original expression of hard impassivity. The easy change made my gorge rise. I wanted to slap away her mask, tear her down into a crying girl again.

"Wait a minute," I said sharply. "How much do I owe you?"

"Owe me?" She looked at me blankly. "You mean, for this?" Her single awkward gesture indicated the bed and her body, the incongruity and pain of the situation.

"How much?"

She had enough character to swallow the pain and master the situation. "I wouldn't take money from you," she said gently.

"But don't you have to pay the management?"

"Sure. I can afford it. But you don't understand. I'd rather starve than take money from you."

"I don't get it." But I got it.

"You don't have to get it." Her eyes went soft as flowers. "You called me lover. You said it as if you meant it."

Mabel's hoarse whisper came through the door: "Can't you hurry up, Carla? Baby here is getting awful impatient."

"I'm coming, hon. Tell baby to keep his shirt on."

"It's not his shirt I'm worried about," Mabel giggled.

We opened the door and passed them in the hall— another tart and another sucker. But on the way downstairs I said to the girl's back: "I meant it." And I did.

Chapter 9

If she answered anything it was drowned out by the renewed blare of the orchestra. She left me at the foot of the stairs, and her white back and shoulders disappeared among the tables like a fading ghost.

There was a bank of slot machines along the wall beside the stairs—a couple of nickel ones for the pikers, dime machines for cautious women, quarter machines for gay couples, fifty-cent machines for big spenders, a massive job with a gullet big enough to swallow a silver dollar for the gamblers and lucky drunks. A few couples and two or three solitary men were working the levers and pouring their money in. A thin youth with the complexion and quick, jumpy movements of a galvanically controlled cadaver roved up and down and made change.

I changed a dollar and tried a quarter machine with a heavy jackpot which had been gestating for a long time. The first two were blanks. The third drew two cherries and a lemon, worth four slugs. I ran my investment up to over three dollars, and the dead-looking youth began to throw interested glances in my direction. He had the evil eye—the machine closed up like a clam and stopped paying. I played in my dozen slugs and got nothing better than two bars with an ironic lemon beside them.

"More quarters, mister?" the youth said.

"Not for me. Business pretty good?"

"Can't complain, I guess. We had some trouble last month with that gang that tried cupping the machines, but we fixed that."

"Call the police?"

"We don't have to call the police, bud. See that guy

sitting by himself over there?" He jerked his thumb toward a heavy curly-haired man at a table by the orchestra. "That's a plain-clothes man the boss keeps handy. Just so there won't be any trouble."

He turned away to change a bill for a nervous drunk.

"I've been wondering if your boss is around," I said. "I'd sort of like to talk to him."

"I saw him go in the back office a while ago. What you want to see him about?"

"I'll tell him. Where's the office?"

He pointed to a door under the stairs. "Through there, down at the end of the hall. It's got his name on it."

There wasn't much light in the hall, but there was enough to read the sign on the door: "R. Kerch, Manager." It was a heavy door, so thick it didn't vibrate under my knuckles. My heart was knocking on my ribs for luck.

"Come in," somebody said.

I opened the door and walked in. It was a low, square room, lit from the ceiling by indirect lighting. It contained a big veneered desk, a few chairs, a heavy safe in a corner fastened to a steel plate that was sunk in the floor, a leather couch against one wall. A big man in shirt sleeves was lying on the couch reading a paper, with his red head propped up on his arm. A shoulder holster hung over the back of the chair beside him.

Kerch was sitting at the desk counting money. His small, white hands moved quickly among sheafs of green bills, like little naked birds in a garden of good things to eat. His wrists bulged out thick above his hands, as if someone had bound his hands and blown air into the rest of him. He was very big behind the desk, and a double-breasted suit of gray gabardine made him look even bigger. A purple silk tie, hand-painted in sunset colors, blossomed at his throat.

Kerch raised his eyes. They came up slowly in his head, as if they had weight and required an effort to lift. They were large, brown eyes with unnaturally wide pupils, which seemed on the point of falling all the way out of his face. The face was broad and flabby, with heavy, bulldog lips. But it was the eyes that gave Kerch his look of soft, infinite malice.

"Yes?" he said. "Is there anything I can do for you?" His voice was carefully modulated and his enunciation, coming from the gross mouth, was surprisingly clear and good.

"I hear you more or less run this town."

"That's an unexpected compliment," he said without expression. It occurred to me that perhaps his face was incapable of expression. "After all, I've been in business here barely two years."

"You seem to be doing all right for yourself." I looked frankly at the piles of money on the table. The man on the couch put down his newspaper and sat up with his feet on the floor.

"Thank you," Kerch said. "Did you come here to discuss my business success with me?"

"In a way. I was told you're a good man to work for—that you paid well, if a man was willing to take a few risks."

"I can't imagine who you've been talking to."

"I've been talking to a few of your employees."

"It was nice of them to put in a good word for me. What sort of risks did you have in mind?"

"Any kind of risk. Life has been pretty dull since I got out of the army."

"And it hasn't been paying so well?" His glance went from my collar down the front of my coat to my scuffed field boots.

"It hasn't been paying at all. I'd like to start in at the bottom of some good lively business and work up."

"I can understand why you might want to work for me," Kerch said. "But what have you got to recommend yourself to me?"

"I'll try anything once. I don't discourage easily. I can fight."

"Can you handle a gun?"

"Yes."

"Rusty, stand up, will you? I'd like to see if this young man can hit you."

Rusty stood up and stretched. He moved away from the couch and crouched forward with his arms hanging loose, his weight on the balls of his feet. He thrust forward his scarred face, which looked rugged enough to break a hand on. His mouth was loose in a playful grin, which showed his broken teeth, but his little eyes, pale-blue slits under brows padded with scar tissue, were watching my feet.

I moved in cautiously and tapped at him with my left to test his speed. He got out of its way without moving his feet, which showed that his speed was fair. But my right cross followed it very quickly and got him on the cheek. While he was off balance my left came back to his jaw and jolted him. Before I could throw another right, he had clinched and began to pound my kidneys with both fists. I broke the clinch and shouldered him heavily. He took two involuntary steps backwards and sat down on his leather couch.

"Stay where you are, Rusty," Kerch said. "I didn't tell you to hurt him. I told you to see if he can hit you. He can."

"He caught me off balance. This punk couldn't lay a finger on me if he didn't catch me off balance." But he didn't get up again.

"I don't want you boys fighting among yourselves," Kerch said. "I like to see a harmonious relationship among my employees."

"Does that mean I've got a job?"

"You should give me one chance at him, Mr. Kerch. You let him hit me."

"You let him hit you, Rusty. He didn't hurt you, did he?"

"Naw, a punk like that couldn't hurt me, even with me giving him the sucker punch."

"Exactly. But if you hit him you'd probably kill him. So, no fighting, please."

Rusty was silent. His battered face caricatured the expression of a small boy who has been refused permission to go to the ball game.

"I said no fighting, please, Rusty."

"No, Mr. Kerch."

Kerch turned to me: "Come and see me at noon tomorrow. I'll be in my suite on the top floor of the Palace. What's your name?"

"John."

"John what?"

"Doe," I said. "My name makes trouble for me."

"Is that so?" Kerch said softly. "Well, John, I think I may be able to give you something to do."

"That's fine."

His swollen eyeballs rotated upwards to look at my face. "By the way, John, my employees usually address me as Mr. Kerch. I'm a little bit of a disciplinarian, you see."

"Yes, Mr. Kerch." The words came out with such difficulty that a lump formed in my throat, but it wasn't the time or place to talk out of turn.

"That's better, John. You may go now."

"Thank you, Mr. Kerch," I said.

I went out the door and down the hall with the blood beating in my head. The door at the end opened before I reached it, and let in a gust of music with Garland walking daintily in the midst of it. We saw each other in the same instant and stood facing in the narrow passage. A swart automatic hopped into his hand like a toad.

"You've certainly got your nerve to come here," Garland said. "Now turn right around and walk to that door at the other end. Kerch will want to see you."

"Aren't you supposed to call him Mr. Kerch?"

"Turn around and move quickly," Garland whined. "You make me impatient."

"You bore me. I don't think you're pretty at all." I took a step towards him.

All the blood ran out of his lips and nostrils, leaving them white and shriveled. "If you come near me I'll fire."

Kerch's door opened behind me, and over my shoulder I caught a glimpse of Rusty coming down the passage.

"Jump him, Rusty," Garland said.

I turned to face the red-headed man who was so big he blocked the hallway from wall to wall. He bore down on me on rapid, shuffling feet, his chin drawn in and a happy snarl wrenching at his face. But I was afraid to hit him because Garland was behind me, balanced precariously on a high, thin peak of hysteria, with a gun.

Rusty swung at me and I stepped back. He swung with his other hand and I moved away again, into the arc of Garland's descending blow. The butt of the gun struck me at the base of the skull and made the floor teeter under my feet. Rusty's third swing made the floor stand up vertically and bounce against the back of my head.

Kerch appeared in his doorway and said: "I told you no fighting, please, Rusty. What are you doing, Garland? Put away that gun."

"You don't know who he is, do you?" Garland chattered. "He's J.D. Weather's son. He came to my flat tonight and made trouble."

I sat up again and looked up into Kerch's bovine face. In spite of his huge head and torso his legs were very short and his feet were tiny. "I'm not surprised you were unwilling to give me your name," he said. His feet moved in an awkward little dancing step and the pointed toe of one caught me under the chin. "I don't like wretched little liars who come to me and try to take advantage of my open-mindedness, worming their way into my good graces."

I tried to speak, but all my throat would produce was a cawing retch. Kerch leaned over me and slapped me twice, with the front and the back of his hand. It didn't hurt me, but it was like being slapped by a dead fish.

"Let me handle him, Mr. Kerch," Rusty said with boyish eagerness.

"Wait a minute. You said he made trouble, Garland?"

"He slugged Joey Sault and tried to make him talk about what happened to his old man. I scared him off."

"Of course Sault didn't talk?"

"He just said that we'd better tell you about it—"

"Now that was unwise, don't you think? Garland, I'd like you to go and get Sault and bring him here."

"He isn't at my flat any more—"

"Go and find him. Rusty, bring this wretched creature into the office." He turned and walked down the hall, wide and foreshortened like a man seen from below.

"Get up, punk," Rusty said, and yanked me by the collar. I got as far as my knees and he cuffed me on the back of the neck. "When I say get up, I mean in a hurry."

I was on my hands and knees in front of him. He raised one foot to step on my fingers. I came up fast underneath him with my head in his crotch, and kept coming up, carrying him off the floor. He let out a yelp of pain and surprise, but swung his legs together, trying to lock a scissors on my neck. I took his ankles, one in each hand, and jerked them apart. Now he was straddling my shoulders, with his body hanging head downwards on my back. I threw myself backwards onto the floor with him under me.

Kerch was watching us around the corner of his door. He made no move to join in the fight. Instead, he took a police whistle out of his pocket and blew once.

Rusty was still under me but his arms were around my waist. Before I could break his hold, a heavy man with curly, black hair came through the door at the end of the hall, moving at a run.

Kerch said: "Arrest this fellow, Moffatt. He came here to try to rob my office."

I had enough voice to croak: "He's a goddam liar."

"Do your duty, Moffatt," Kerch said. "Surely the two of you can handle him."

Rusty had twisted under me and had my throat in the crook of his elbow. I reached for his wrist with both hands to bend his arm away. Moffatt sat down on my chest and put handcuffs on me.

"Get the hell off," Rusty said in a muffled voice. "I'm under here."

Moffatt stood up and yanked me to my feet. "Do I take him down and book him, Mr. Kerch?"

"Bring him into the office."

We all went into the office. Kerch hid his short legs under the desk. I stood in front of him like a prisoner at the bar, Moffatt and Rusty on either side of me.

"What charges you want to make, Mr. Kerch?" Moffatt said.

"I've been thinking about that. He'd be good for attempted robbery and aggravated assault."

"Resisting an officer in the performance of his duty? Assault with a deadly weapon while attempting to commit a robbery?"

"On the other hand, I wouldn't wish to be too hard on him, Moffatt. He's young. He may have a future, though God knows that's doubtful. And after all, he didn't get away with anything, thanks to you."

"I was holding him, Mr. Kerch," Rusty said anxiously. "He couldn't get away from me."

"I'll talk to you later, Rusty."

"What do I do with him, Mr. Kerch?" Moffatt said.

"Take him down the highway, about three miles, I think. Start him walking in the direction of Chicago. I don't believe he'll want to come back and face the charges."

"You certainly are a pretty generous guy, Mr. Kerch. Personally, I don't think a few days in the cells would do him any harm."

"Perhaps not, Moffatt. But I was young once myself. I wouldn't want this boy's life to be shadowed by a term in jail. Have you ever been in jail, son?"

"No," I said.

"You'll be careful not to come back, then. If you should happen to come back, you can expect to spend ten years in jail. I'm not exaggerating, nor am I bluffing. You may go now, Moffatt."

"Yes, Mr. Kerch."

He took me out a back door to the parking lot, and opened the door of his black police car for me. His hat was on the seat, and he put it on and slid behind the wheel. The car moved down the gravel drive and turned into the highway.

"You don't know how lucky you are," the plain-clothes man said. "If you knew enough to keep your nose clean, you wouldn't go messing around with Kerch. He's a big man in these parts."

"I can see that."

"He gave you a real break. You want to remember that. This is your chance to straighten out, kid."

"Yeah. From now on I'm going straight. Mr. Kerch has certainly made me see the light. How about taking these bracelets off me?"

"Don't worry. I'll take 'em off when you get out. Those things cost money."

The speedometer moved up to sixty and stayed there. The wind came through the half-open window and blew the hair around on my sick head.

"I'll let you off near Section Corner," Moffatt said. "You can maybe pick up a ride at Sid's Hamburg. A lot of trucks stop there."

"You're very kind."

"Hell, don't mention it."

A minute later he stopped the car and leaned across me to open the door. "You can get out now."

"What about these handcuffs?"

"I'm getting out, too."

I stepped out and stood on the soft shoulder of the road. About half a mile up the highway I could see the green traffic signal at a crossroads. Moffatt got out behind me and reached in his pocket as if for his keys. Then something swished through the air. All the stars fell down and the night turned solid black.

I came to in a dry ditch beside the highway. The stars had returned to the sky, higher and brighter than ever. The handcuffs had been removed from my wrists, and the police car was gone.

Another car came sliding down its groove of light towards me, and I stood up and waved with both arms. It passed me as indifferently as it would have passed a scarecrow in a field.

I felt for my wallet and found it where it should be,

but there was no money in it. I had nothing left but some change in my watch pocket.

I climbed back onto the road and started walking towards the city. The reflection of its neons hung a faint rosy glow in the sky, as if I was walking back into the suburbs of hell.

Chapter 10

I left the highway at the first crossing, so as not to pass the Cathay Club again. On one side of the road there was a patch of woods, identified by a sign as Dingle Dell Developments, Inc. On other side there was a scattering of houses, new and pretentious, with built-in two-car garages, high, tiled roofs, and leaded windows. All the windows were dark, but a dog behind one of the houses woke up and barked at me as I went by. I hated the smug, sleeping occupants of those closed houses. At the same time there was a strong wish deep in my mind to be safe in bed behind one of the blinded windows, with a plump wife to keep me warm.

There was a bus-stop sign at the next corner, and I sat down on a concrete bench and waited. Down the road towards the city I could see a lighted ferris wheel turning in the sky. After a while a bus appeared from the direction of the city and turned around at the corner. I got on and slumped in a seat behind the driver.

He said: "Pretty nice night for this early in the spring, eh, bud?"

"Yeah, and pretty soon the bunny will be bringing Easter eggs besides."

He gave me a startled look over his shoulder and dropped me from his mind. My consciousness began to operate in fits and starts, like a bored conversation, and finally blanked out in sleep. I woke up momentarily when the bus stopped and filled up with passengers at the amusement park. They climbed in, laughing and talking and yelling drunkenly:—an apprentice seaman clutching a papier-mâché doll in one hand and a girl in the other; a couple of sleek youngsters in zoot suits, sharing a girl with precocious breasts and a dopey look on her face; an obvious floozie with purple eyelids, embraced by a tall, pale boy whose forehead was shining with sweat; a little man who wanted to fight, being soothed by a larger companion; a sleepy young man in an imitation llama coat, accompanied by a henna redhead and a peroxide blonde.

He stopped beside me and leaned over clumsily: "Say, haven't I seen you somewhere before?"

"Never," I said. "I just arrived from South Africa where my father owns the Kimberley Diamond Mines. His name, curiously enough, is Jan Christian Smuts."

"That a fact?" said the sleepy young man. He looked at me in sudden horror, doubled up, and vomited on the floor.

"Gracious Jesus!" the driver said. "Do I have to ride with the smell again all night?"

"I'm sorry, Christ, I'm sorry," the young man said. He took a figured silk scarf from around his neck and got down on his knees to wipe the floor.

I pushed back in my corner and went to sleep again. A man with a changing face followed me down a street that I knew well. I was only a young kid and he frightened me. It was dark and growing darker. I came to the mouth of an alley and ran into it, scurrying silently between blind brick walls. A door opened in the wall and I slammed it shut before the man could catch me. The moose head and the hall tree were there, and I climbed the stairs to my own room. But the room was full of unfriendly faces, jostling and pushing towards me. I ran down the hall to my father's room, calling to him to come and help me. The room was empty, the windows were broken, the bed was covered with dust. A smiling rat hopped out of the abandoned bed and ran between my legs, brushing me with his tail.

I woke up with tears wet on my face. The bus was nearly empty, and the last few passengers were standing in line in the aisle, waiting to get out.

"Can you tell me where the Mayor lives?" I asked the driver.

"Yeah, he lives here on the north side. I don't know exactly where. You can ask them in the terminal."

Another bus took me within a couple of blocks of Allister's address, and I got out and walked the rest of the way. It was a white frame colonial house, with decorative green shutters opening at the sides of the windows. There were no lights on, but I went up the red brick walk, climbed the shallow porch, and knocked on the door with its bronze lion's head.

In a minute the light on the porch came on, then the light in the hall inside. Slippered feet shuffled down the stairs into the hall, the lock was snapped back, and the door opened. A thin man in his late thirties, with nervous lines in his face, peered out at me.

"Mr. Allister?"

"What do you want?" His graying hair was rumpled, and his eyes were bleared with sleep.

"I want help—"

"My God, you people never give me any rest! Look, you can get a free bed down at the Center. They'll give you breakfast in the morning." He started to close the door.

"Not that kind of help. I'm J.D. Weather's son. You must have known my father."

"J.D. Weather didn't have a son." He looked into my face suspiciously.

I pulled out my wallet and showed him the photostat of my discharge papers. "You can see my name's Weather. I want to talk to you—"

"What about? This is a hell of a time of night to wake me up."

"I was told that you're an honest man."

"Come in," he said then, and opened the door wide. I stepped in and followed him down the hall. "We'll go into the den."

A plain camel's-hair bathrobe tied with a rope gave his thin shoulders and back a monkish look. The impression of monastic austerity was continued in his den, which was as sparsely furnished as a monk's cell. A solid table with a typewriter on it, a wire basket full of papers, a straight chair in front of it, a leather armchair to one side by the window, the walls lined with shelves of books. When he turned on the green-shaded desk lamp I noticed some of the titles: *Civil Statutes,* Parrington's *Main Currents of American Thought,* William James's *Psychology,* Malraux's *La Condition Humaine.*

He motioned me into the armchair, turned the straight chair away from the table, and sat down facing me. His face was lean and intelligent, with a strong brow and a sensitive mouth. His nose was thin, but his nostrils were heavily winged and flared when he breathed like a race horse's. His blue eyes were steady, but their gaze was clouded by something. I suspected that he saw the world through a haze of dreamy idealism. A strange man, I thought, to become a successful politician in such a city.

"Well," he said, "what can I do for you?"

"Maybe I can do something for you. This is the way I see it—correct me if I'm wrong. You ran for Mayor on a reform platform and got in, probably to your own surprise. But once you were in the City Hall you found out that it wasn't so easy to clean up the city. Corruption was solidly intrenched and backed by powerful interests. You had to welch on your promise to the decent people that supported you—"

"The city government was an Augean stable," he said with a doleful smile. "But you didn't come here in the middle of the night to tell me that."

"I don't know how much you've been able to do, but it looks to me as if it still is. I know the police are a bloody scandal—I had my pocket picked by one of them tonight."

"Can you give me the man's name? I'm on the police board—"

"I'm not interested in pointing out one man to you. The whole force is rotten. In spite of the fact that you've been on the police board for nearly two years."

"I've done what I could," Allister said soberly. "You don't know the situation. You've got to remember that I'm a minority of one on the police board. The other members are appointed by the city council, and I don't control the city council. I've tried more than once to force through a full-scale investigation of the police. I've got enough evidence in my files to turn the whole department upside down. But the council blocked me. Most of them have been bought."

"Why don't you appeal directly to the voters?"

"I'm going to." He leaned forward tensely. "But I have to fight the council with their own weapons. If I come out in the open too soon, they'll get together to defeat me in the next election, and that'll be the end of municipal reform. I can't afford to act now, with the election coming up in April. But I'm building up a machine that will beat them at their own game. The people are learning that I'm on their side."

He settled back and took a deep breath, like an orator drinking a glass of water between paragraphs. His blue gaze rested on my face, clearing suddenly as if he were seeing me now for the first time.

"It's queer that I should be talking like this to J.D. Weather's son." He smiled the formal smile of a humorless man. "Municipal reform isn't exactly part of your family tradition."

"Don't start telling me that my father dirtied this town. Apparently he did his share, but one man can't corrupt a town all by himself. It takes co-operation."

"You're right, Weather. I saw that only too clearly after your father died. You've got to realize that he and I were political enemies for years. I fought him when I was in Cranbridge in the D.A.'s office, and I fought him when I came back here to run for the council. I began to feel that one man was holding back this town, and that he was the man. But I was wrong. He died and things went on as before. It wasn't a man I had to fight—it was a system. There were always others to take his place." He lowered his head in a slightly actorish gesture.

"Kerch, for instance," I said. "My father was a saint compared with R. Kerch."

"I never denied in private that J.D. had his virtues," Allister said. "But this Kerch is evil through and through. I'd give anything to have this town rid of him." There was a faint note of unreality in everything he said, as if the true nature of the world had always escaped him. But his face and his whole body were passionately sincere.

I said: "You don't have to give anything. Lend me fifty dollars and a gun."

"I can let you have some money," he said slowly. "But I haven't a gun. Why do you want a gun?"

"For self-protection. I'm going to kill Kerch with my bare hands, and I'll need a gun for self-protection while I'm doing it."

He looked shocked. "You're not serious?"

"I'm dead serious. You think the town would be better off without him. You can't touch him yourself, but you want to get rid of him. This is your chance. Get me a gun."

"What you're proposing is murder." He jumped up quickly and walked back and forth across the room. "And you're asking me to be an accessory to it."

"Murder is nothing new to this town."

"Is Kerch a murderer? Is that what you mean?"

"My father was murdered, and Kerch took over his business. If Kerch didn't do it himself, he got somebody to do it for him."

He stood still in the center of the room and faced me. He looked harried and distraught, his thin face and body worn down fine by the friction of an environment that was too rough for him: "You don't realize what you're proposing, Weather. You couldn't even get to Kerch. He never goes anywhere without a bodyguard. Even if you did, you'd never get away."

"I'll take my chance. The only chance I'm asking you to take is one on me. And you can count on me. If I'm caught, I won't talk about you."

"I don't like this," he said uncertainly.

"I don't expect you to like it. But you said yourself that evil has to be fought with its own weapons. Can you get me a gun?"

Determination crystallized slowly in his eyes. He bit his lip. "Wait here," he said finally.

He stepped into the hall and closed the door behind him. I heard him lift a telephone receiver and ask for a number: 23748. After that his voice was too low for me to hear anything but scattered words. Twice he said gun.

Then he slammed down the receiver and thrust his head in at the door. He spoke quickly as if rapid speech and action could shake off the doubts that nagged at his face:

"Wait here. I'll have to get dressed and go out for a minute. Read a book if you like."

"I'm not in the mood for reading. Can you get me one?"

"Yes. I think so. In my profession, you know, you make contacts with all sorts of people. I'll be back in fifteen or twenty minutes." He withdrew his head with the suddenness of a startled gopher, and ran up the stairs, two at a time. A few minutes later I heard him come down and leave the house.

Allister was a queer duck, I thought, but he had his points. Not everyone would leave a total stranger alone in his house at night. And he had gone much further than that—gone out of his way to provide me with the one thing I needed to go on living in the same town with Kerch. He hated Kerch as sincerely as I did, and though he didn't seem to have much physical courage, he had moral daring. In spite of his position, he had the daring to step outside the law for a purpose that seemed good to him. He wasn't my type at all, but I felt respect and affection for him, as if he were at the same time both my older and my younger brother. The idealism that made him seem unrealistic and a little silly was the thing in him that I knew I could depend on, because he was a man ruled by general ideas. In a way he reminded me of Kaufman, the radical who sat in the back of his secondhand shop like an old spider, too disinterested to catch flies.

My mind skipped from Kaufman to his granddaughter Carla. Where would she be in five years? What would she be doing? How did she feel about me? Would I ever see her again? Probably, because I certainly seemed to be getting around. It didn't occur to me that I could ever die.

The night had passed its three o'clock crisis, and the patch of earth where the city stood was turning now not away from evening but towards morning. An hour before, I had felt almost finished, beaten down and about ready to quit. Since then a tide had turned in my blood. My head was light and sore, but I felt ready to fight the city again. I waited for Allister impatiently. I wanted to be on my way.

I lit a cigarette, the first I had remembered to smoke all night. But the smoke I drew into my lungs had a predawn bitterness. I crushed it out in the bottom of a steel wastebasket. There were no ashtrays in the room.

Then I heard hurrying footsteps coming up the walk to the porch, and the front door opening. I opened the door of the den, and Allister trotted in, wearing a gray pin-stripe suit and a fedora. He closed the door behind him with a conspiratorial gesture that made me smile to myself.

"Did you get it?"

He brought his hand out of the pocket of his outer coat, holding a heavy automatic by the muzzle. "I hope you know how to work an automatic, because I don't. Be careful how you handle it. It's loaded."

I took it from him and saw that it was a Colt .45. I slid out the clip and ran my fingers over the copper-headed bullets nestling together like peas in a pod. I dropped it in my pocket, where it made a reassuring weight.

"I can use it. Have you got any extra shells?"

He handed me a small cardboard box which dragged down my other pocket. There was a confused gleam in his eyes, as if he was frightening himself but was pleased and surprised by his own temerity.

"And I need some money. My pockets were cleaned out."

He took out an alligator billfold and counted out five tens. "If you need more, you can come to me," he said. "But if you get into trouble, it wouldn't do to bring me into it. It wouldn't help you, and it would do me a terrible lot of harm. You understand that, don't you?"

"I told you you could count on me. I'll send back your money when I can."

"Forget about it. I don't need it. But you won't send the gun back, will you?"

"If it does what I hope it will, I'll have to ditch it anyway."

He opened the front door for me and gave me his slender hand in a rigid boy-scout grip. "Good luck. Take care of yourself."

"I think I can, now," I said. "I won't forget your help."

I went down the walk to the dark street and turned towards the center of town.

Chapter 11

I walked on tree-lined sidewalks beside broad lawns for five or six blocks, cut across a triangle of public park, and abruptly found myself in the slums again. They seemed to form a circular zone which surrounded the heart of the city, as if the money that was concentrated in the downtown banks and business houses was thrown outward by centrifugal force, skipping the rundown areas around the center and enriching the periphery. Now there were no more lawns and no more trees. The massed tenements shouldered in to the street and narrowed the sky. A drunk was sleeping noisily in a doorway, and in another a pair of dispossessed lovers possessed what they could of each other against the wall.

An all-night restaurant in the next block reminded me that I hadn't eaten since noon the day before. There were no customers, and I went in and slid into an enclosed booth at the back.

"A couple of fried eggs," I told the young man in the dirty apron who dabbled halfheartedly at my table with a wet rag.

"No eggs. All I got is fish and chips."

"Make it fish and chips."

He shuffled away, as if sleepiness was an element he waded through all night. My table was covered with checkered brown oilcloth, worn threadbare by many threadbare elbows. At the end of the table against the wall were a glass canister of sugar with a pouring spout, a bottle of vinegar, salt and pepper, and an unlabeled bottle of ketchup with a bloody mouth. A cockroach stepped out from behind the ketchup, gave me a quick impassive once-over, decided that I was of the

Brahmin faith, and walked earnestly across the table on errands of his own. Somebody had left a newspaper on the bench beside me, and I picked it up and swatted the cockroach, permitting his soul to transmigrate into the body of a quartermaster.

The paper had been left open at the editorial page, and the title of one of the editorials caught my eye: "Our City, an Example to the Nation." I read idly down the column:

During recent months this country as a whole has been swept by an unprecedented wave of disastrous labor troubles. In city after city, industry after industry, organized labor under the leadership of foreign-born Reds and terrorists, has broken its pledged word to the American people and forced strikes and violence on our industrial leaders, who have thus been interrupted in their great task of reconverting the country's factories to peacetime production. Organized labor has made a mockery of the hopes of our returning veterans for peace and security. They have come back from the bloody fields of France and Okinawa to find not peace but a sword, disrupted production schedules resulting in shortages of essential goods, wasted man-hours, anarchy where there should be discipline, the blood of their brothers running in the streets under the bludgeons of gangs of terrorists.

We can praise God and the foresight of our local leaders that the life of our fair city has not been blighted and blasted by C. I. O. threats and Communist violence. Nearly two years ago, in May 1944, while Armageddon was still upon us and our industries were straining every nerve to win the battle of production, our city fathers, led by that grand old man of municipal life, Alonzo P. Sanford, and our newly elected Mayor, Freeman Allister, foresaw the danger of labor violence and nipped it in the bud. At that time, under cover of wartime manpower needs and the fatuous favoritism of the Administration, C. I. O. agitators, Communistic-minded propagandists, and other dissident elements had infiltrated our local industries, attempting to lay the groundwork for future disruptive and revolutionary activities, such as we see today in other parts of the country. But the guardians of our municipal virtue were vigilant and alert. With the efficient co-operation of our excellent police force, the agitators who would have sabotaged our contribution to the national effort were weeded out and properly dealt with. Ours was one city that had a citizenry intelligent enough to perceive the dangers ahead, and a municipal government courageous enough to act to avert them in time.

As a result we can claim without false pride that the local industrial area is one of the few zones of quiet in the chaotic labor situation which overspreads the country. And let no moon-struck visionaries of the Wallace type claim that our city is antilabor. Our armies of cheerful and well-trained workers, organized under local and truly American auspices in independent unions that protect all their rights as individuals, would be the first to laugh such an idea to utter scorn.

Ours is the American way. We offer our shining example, which shines like a good deed in a naughty world, as the Bard says, to a distraught nation torn by violence and industrial strife. Our local Chamber of Commerce welcomes inquiries from new businesses, or from old firms seeking a new location, which are interested in the possibilities of a disciplined and patriotic labor supply on the doorstep of the great markets of the Middle West.

"Pretty hot stuff, eh, Mac?" the waiter said over my shoulder. "I read that one myself."

"You liked it?"

"Don't kid me." He set my plate in front of me and spat on the floor. "My old man and my old lady worked out at Sanford's for the last thirty years. They're gettin' old now, and they make less than they did when they started. My brother was there for a while, till they broke his elbow with a lead pipe and threw him out of town. He was one of the foreign agitators they were talkin' about in this story in the paper. If Bobby was a Communist, I'm Uncle Joe Stalin with bells on."

"How does the story go over with people in general?"

"Those that want to believe it, believe it." He gave me a knife and fork and pulled the vinegar into the center of the table. "Practically everybody that's got any money in the bank and thinks he can squeeze some more. And all the goddam little bank clerks and salesmen and stenographers that go around suckholing their bosses. The rest of us take it for the crap it is. Christ, everybody knows who owns the paper."

"Sanford?"

"You're a good guesser. Coffee?"

"Yeah."

"With or without?"

"With."

He brought me coffee in a thick white cup, and shuffled away again.

When I was swallowing the last of my fish and chips, the door of the restaurant opened and somebody came in. On general principles I slumped down in my seat so that my head wouldn't show over the back of the booth. It was just as well I did that, because the voice I heard was Joe Sault's:

"You can give me that brief case now."

"You're damn right I can," the waiter replied. "You think I like keeping stuff like that under the counter?"

"I don't know what you're talking about. Everybody in the insurance business carries a brief case, don't he? I got a right to carry a brief case, don't I?"

"So now you're selling insurance? If the cops found that thing in here, it'd fix me."

"No cop interferes with my business." A coin rolled on the counter. "Here. Buy yourself a syringe and keep your nose clean."

"Yeah," the waiter grumbled. "That goes for everybody, Sault."

"Mr. Sault to you, eh?" The door opened and closed.

"To hell with you, Joey," the waiter said to himself.

I leaned around the corner of my booth and made sure that Sault was clear of the windows. On the way out I flipped the waiter a half and told him to keep the change.

From the doorway I saw Sault pass under a street

light halfway down the block, walking jauntily with his
black brief case swinging beside him. I followed him at
the same pace until he had turned the corner, then
walked faster to shorten the distance between us. When
I reached the corner, he was about two hundred yards
ahead of me, headed downhill towards Main Street.

I didn't want to go downtown, where my friends the
police were concentrated, but I decided to follow Sault.
Perhaps he would lead me to Kerch, or to somebody
else I'd like to know better. I could have caught him
and tried to make him talk, but that had failed before.
I was losing faith in the direct approach. And now that
I had a gun I felt I could afford to wait a little.

At the next corner he went straight on across the
street and down the next block. I crossed to the other
side and moved up on him, ready to duck into a doorway if he turned his head. There were few pedestrians
on the streets and even fewer cars, but Sault swaggered
for his own benefit as if he were walking among admir-
ing crowds at high noon, the local boy who had made
good.

Someone tapped lightly on a first-floor window just
above my head, and I recoiled as if a gun had popped.
It was only a late whore holding out her heavy breast
the way a butcher holds up a steak for the customer's
approval. I wagged my head and she jerked down her
blind to keep out peeping toms.

A woman with a streetwalker's jaded lilt in her step
approached Sault from the opposite direction and
stopped him under a street light. She put her hand on his
arm in a gesture of appeal, but he brushed it off. She
lifted her skirt, dug into the top of her stocking, and
showed him something in her hand. He jerked his head
in my direction, and I slid into the mouth of an alley-
way. They crossed the street towards me, Sault walking
ahead and the woman trailing along behind like a Ger-
man wife. They seemed to be headed for my alley, and
I retreated with my hand around the butt of my gun.

I squatted against the wall behind a big paper carton
and heard the two sets of footsteps, one heavy and as-

sured, the other quick and uncertain, coming down the alley towards me.

"O.K., Gert," Sault said, "put up and you can have it. No money, no smokey."

They had stopped before they came to me, and stood together in the faint light that reached them from the street. Their shadows lay along the dirty concrete in front of me, enlarged to heroic size. The woman's shadow raised its elongated hand to its tall head, posed like a baroque saint in agony.

"I can pay you for what you give me now," she said urgently. "If I pay you for last week, I won't have any money left."

"Sure you will, Gert. You can always make some money, a fine girl like you."

"I want to go home," she whispered. "I been pounding the pavements since eight o'clock. Give me a break, Joey. I couldn't get to sleep for three nights now."

"I want to give you a break. I'd love to give you a break. But I got expenses to meet, remember that. I don't have capital to carry my friends on the cuff."

She spoke now with a deathly coquetry, and her shadow huddled towards him. "If you give me just one, you could come home with me. I got to keep a buck to eat tomorrow. You used to like me, Joey."

"Did I? Maybe I did. But I don't pay for it, kid. Hell, sometimes I get paid."

"Please, Joey."

He pushed her away, and her shadow staggered soundlessly across the alley. I had a childish impulse to play Robin Hood, to hold him up and give her all the marijuana in the brief case. But in the long run it wouldn't do her any good, and it wouldn't do me any good at all.

"I got no more time to waste, Gert," he said sharply. "Pay me the four dollars from last week and I'll sell you two, cash on the line."

"All right, you dirty Shylock."

His shadow jerked and started to walk away.

"Joey, where are you going?" she cried in sudden terror. "Don't go away. Come back. Please."

"Pretty please. And I like you to call me Mr. Sault."

"Pretty please," she said desperately. "Mr. Sault."

"And five bucks, eh?"

She went to him humbly and gave him what was in her hand. He clicked open the brief case and handed her a little package wrapped in newspaper. I watched them over the edge of the carton.

"Now thank me," Sault said. "I didn't like your crack."

"Thank you, Mr. Sault," she said, in a voice breaking with hatred and relief. "Thank you, Mr. Sault. Thank you, Mr. Sault."

He turned on his heel and walked down the alley. She followed him like a vicious she-dog who hates and fears her master, still mouthing her thanks. Their shadows stalked them out, hardening and shrinking to life-size as they emerged into the street. The woman went one way and Sault went the other, walking more jauntily than ever. I followed Sault.

One block north of Main Street he turned left on West Mack. I crossed the street as soon as he was out of sight and came up to the corner cautiously. A block away on Main Street I caught sight of a policeman dawdling under a street light, but he paid no attention to me. When I looked around the corner in the direction Sault had taken, he had disappeared.

A hundred yards down the block a woman came out of a doorway, her raddled face lit into brief rosy youth by a red neon sign over her head which said, "Full Course Italian Dinners." She hobbled mincingly towards me on high heels, and I went to meet her.

"Lonesome, friend?" she said as we passed.

"Yeah. I like to be lonesome."

"O.K.," she said wearily. "I was just asking." She went on up the block like a sick old bird with a drooping tail.

I looked into the restaurant window, past a boiled lobster and a big plaster sundae on which generations of flies had left their marks, and saw Sault's profile in a phone booth. He seemed to be arguing excitedly, like a man being asked to do something he didn't want to do.

I moved away from the window and walked back to the corner to wait for him. In another minute he came out of the restaurant without his brief case, and walked rapidly in my direction. I left the corner, jumped into the first doorway I came to, and flattened myself against the door inside a triangle of shadow. He passed me on quick feet, his eyes fixed straight ahead in gloomy concentration.

I gave him a slow count of fifty, and stepped out of the doorway. He had almost reached the next corner. I recrossed the street and hurried after him, staying close enough to keep him in sight and far enough away to be unrecognizable if he turned around. He went straight on uphill towards the north-side residential section. Up Lillian Street to West Farmer, across the little park at Farmer's Square, around the corner at the First Presbyterian Church, and up Fenton Boulevard. We were coming into the streets where I had played when I was a kid, and all their names came back to me of their own accord. I passed the iron fence I used to vault over into the churchyard, and noticed how much lower it seemed.

Once we got on Fenton Boulevard, which was lined with elms and maples, it was easy to keep him in sight without being seen myself, though I had to stretch my legs to keep up with him. His broad-brimmed fedora and dark, form-fitting topcoat moved ahead of me down a corridor of trees, alternately lighted and shadowed. The pace he set made me breathe noticeably, but the chase took on a dreamlike quality, as if we were hustling down dark streets that existed only in my own mind. I had the irrational nightmare suspicion that I was hunting a man who was hunting another who would turn out to be me.

I noticed a house I had trespassed in when it was being built, and written my name in the wet plaster. It didn't look like a new house any more. When I looked back to the street Sault was gone.

I stepped off the sidewalk onto the spongy lawns and

ran after him. A long, black car crawled down a side street and turned the corner ahead of me in the direction Sault had gone. I instinctively stopped behind a bush, and, when the car passed under a street light, I knew why. Garland was at the wheel.

Two houses up from the corner a front door opened suddenly and threw a shaft of light across the porch where Sault was standing. He stepped inside and the door closed behind him.

Garland's car crawled up the boulevard and out of sight. I stood in the dark, wondering about several things. I wondered, for example, why Joe Sault should go to my father's house to visit my stepmother at four o'clock in the morning.

Chapter 12

The street was empty now, and I went back to the sidewalk and along it to the house that Sault had entered. There was light in the front room where Mrs. Weather had entertained me, but the tightly drawn curtains cut it off almost completely. The side windows of the room were equally well curtained, so that there was not a chink to see through. I thought of trying the front door, but decided against it. Even if it was unlocked, which was unlikely, I could hardly get in without being heard or seen from the front room. I went around to the back.

The service entrance at the side was locked, and so was the back door which led to the kitchen. I tried the kitchen windows; they were all firmly shut. But nothing had been changed at the back of the house. I sat down on the bottom step of the kitchen stoop and took off my boots and socks. I stuffed the socks into the toes of the boots, which I hung around my neck by their strings. Then I went around to the laundry cistern at the back of the stoop. The grass was chilly and ticklish on the naked soles of my feet.

I took hold of the drainpipe that emptied into the cistern, and pulled hard. It seemed steady, but I doubted whether it would hold my weight. It had when I was twelve, more than once, but I had weighed half as much then. Still, I had had a good deal of practice in house-to-house fighting since then. If the drainpipe wasn't rotten with rust I should be able to make it.

I went up hand over hand, bracing my back against the kitchen stoop, which formed a right angle with the rear wall of the house. The thin pipe groaned in my fingers, but I was high enough now to support some of my weight with my foot on a windowsill. An ornamental row of bricks, which projected slightly above the window, gave me my next foothold. I couldn't see what I was doing, but I was surprised to find that I didn't need to. I had done it before in the dark, and muscles have a long memory.

Sweat was wetting my undershirt and the muscles in my arms were starting to go dead when I finally got hold of the railing that ran around the second-story porch. For a moment I hung suspended, one hand on the drainpipe and the other on the railing, with the concrete lid of the cistern fifteen feet below me in the dark. I didn't trust the railing to bear my weight, but I had to or quit. I swung my other hand onto the railing and started to pull myself over. It creaked and gave, but held me. I drew myself up and stepped over onto the porch.

The outside screen door was locked, as it always had been, with a simple hook. I slit the screen with Sault's spring knife and let myself into the house. The inner door had never had a key.

There was a dim night light burning in the newel post at the head of the front stairs, enough to give me my bearings. I unslung my boots, left them on the top step, and went down the back stairs to the kitchen. Nineteen steps, with a ninety-nine degree turn at the tenth step and a closed door at the bottom, which my fingers anticipated. I caught myself wondering if the refrigerator was still in the same corner of the kitchen.

The swinging door between the kitchen and the dining-room was standing open. I found it with my hands and went through on tiptoe. The only noise I made came from my heart, which pounded in my ears like rapid surf.

The sliding doors which separated the front room from the dining-room were imperfectly closed. A wafer of light came through between them and made a bright band across the dining-room table. I could hear low voices in the next room.

I took the automatic out of my pocket and pushed off the safety, holding it between thumb and forefinger so that it wouldn't click. Walking heel and toe I crossed the carpet to the doors and peered through. All I could see was an empty section of floor, part of an armchair with nobody in it, a shadowy curtain. But I could hear what the voices were saying. They must be in the chesterfield to the right of the door, I thought.

"I can't see why you're so scared of this boy Weather," Sault said. "He tried some rough stuff on me, but it didn't take me long to get rid of him. He slunk away like a yellow dog with his tail between his legs."

"You're a man," Mrs. Weather said softly. "You know how to handle people like that—"

"O.K., so what you want me to do for you? Run him out of town? I can do that."

She continued her own train of thought: "It isn't that I'm so much afraid of anything he'll do to me directly. He threatened me last night—"

"He did, did he? Why the hell didn't you call me up? I wouldn't've let him get away so easy."

"I did call you. I've been trying to get in touch with you all night. I told you that."

"Yeah. You know the boy to come to when you want something done, eh, Floraine?"

"You're sweet, Joey. I feel ever so much better, now that you're here."

For a while there was nothing but silence, broken finally by the slow ending of a kiss.

"You're hot stuff, baby," Sault said throatily. "It's about time you decided to give me another break."

"Don't, Joey. You take my breath away. I've got to talk to you."

"Don't look so gorgeous then. How can I sit here and not do anything with you looking so gorgeous?"

"Listen to me, Joey." Her voice was quick and cool again. "John Weather threatened my life, but it's not him I'm afraid of. I don't think he's got the guts to do anything. He's a wild talker, though, and I'm afraid he can make trouble. His father had some good friends in this town, and he'll go to them and talk about me."

"So what? Talking won't hurt you. Nobody's got anything on you."

"Maybe not," she said uncertainly. After a pause: "Joey, you said you wanted me to give you another break?"

"You know I go for you. It wasn't any fun for me when you cut me off."

"I had to, darling. Don't you see? Everybody in town was watching me after the old man died. I couldn't afford to take any chances."

"But now you can afford to take chances? I don't get it."

Her voice had risen a full octave when she spoke again: "I've got to take a chance. A big chance. I can't go on like this any longer."

"Looks to me as if you're sitting pretty."

"Sitting pretty?" She laughed shallowly. "I'm sitting pretty on the rim of a volcano. I've never told anybody, Joey. Not even you."

"This Weather guy," Sault said slowly. "He got something on you?"

"Not yet. I'm afraid he will."

"What's he going to get on you, baby? Tell your Uncle Joey."

"He won't get anything if you'll help me. If you'll help me, we'll both be sitting pretty for the rest of our lives."

"You know I'll help you, baby. Help you do what?"

"You've got a gun, haven't you?"

"Sure. Not with me, but I can get one." A little whine threaded the masculine assurance of his voice. "I don't like working with guns, Floraine. I can get away with most things in this town, but not murder."

"You can get away with murder, too. I'm asking you to take a chance, Joey, but I'm offering you the big break of your life. We'll both be in it together, and we'll work together from now on. Everything I've got, I'll split with you fifty-fifty."

"For wiping out this John Weather? I'll do it."

"Not John Weather, Joey. If you do what I want

you to do, he can never touch me. I want you to kill
Kerch."

"Kerch?" Surprise and terror plucked simultaneously
at his vocal cords, and turned the harsh syllable into a
squawk.

"You've got to kill Roger Kerch," she said evenly.

"But I thought you and Kerch was like that? My
God, Floraine!"

"Are you afraid?"

"Me? Afraid?" His voice cracked. "You know I'm
not afraid. I'm just surprised, that's all. I always heard
that you and Kerch were—you know, pretty good
friends." The way he said it, "friends" was as obscene
as any four-letter word.

"Somebody's been kidding you. I can't stand him."

"He's got something on you, eh?"

"That's right, Joey. For the last two years, ever since
he came here, I haven't had a moment's peace. Will
you help me?" The range and complexity of her voice
fascinated me. It had purred like a cat in passion, cut
like whips in scorn, teetered on the edge of hysteria,
sunk low in maternal solicitude. Now she was a little
girl again, appealing to his masculine strength. "Will
you help me, Joey?" she repeated.

He answered her with difficulty: "I can't kill him,
Floraine. He keeps Garland and Rusty with him all the
time. If I did, I got no protection for that kind of a
rap. He's in solid with the cops."

"He won't be when he's dead, Joey. He'll be nothing
but cold meat when you step into his shoes. You take
over the Cathay Club and the machines, and the cops'll
know which side their bread is buttered on. They follow the graft, and you'll be the man that's handing it
out."

"You want me to take over the club and the machines?" His voice was incredulous. "Jesus!"

"You're the only man I'd trust," she said earnestly.
"If you'll work with me, we can go places. You're too
big a man to spend your life in the small time. I can
see that, even if you can't."

"Yeah, I know," he admitted. "I been marking time, waiting for a break."

"This is the break you've been waiting for. You can be top man in this town. Will you do it?"

"I'll do it," he said in a shy voice. "By Jesus Christ, I'll do it!"

"I knew I could depend on you."

There was another pause, ending in a long female sigh. "I love you, Joey."

"You know how I feel about you, baby."

"Can you get a gun today?"

"Yeah. But I was thinking. What about Rusty and Garland? When one of them isn't with him, the other one is."

"Leave Rusty to me," she said. "I've seen the way he looks at me. I'll give you a clear field. There's one other thing you've got to do."

"Yeah? What's that?"

"You've seen the safe in Kerch's office at the club?"

"Yeah."

"There's an envelope in it with my name on it. He showed it to me once. You've got to get it."

"Christ, I can't do that. I've never cracked a safe."

"But you don't have to crack it. I own the club. When Kerch is dead, I've got a right to open that safe. We can get a locksmith to drill it open. But you've got to get that envelope before anybody else gets it."

"I'll get it," he said. "What's he got on you, Floraine?"

"I can't tell you now."

"You don't trust me, eh? I thought we were working together now. Tell me what he's got on you, Floraine."

"I'll tell you when he's dead."

"It might take a while. I got to make plans, especially when I'm working in the dark like this."

"It's got to be today. You said today."

"The hell I did. It could take a week for me to get a chance at him. I've got to think about a getaway, too."

"I said I'd take care of Rusty and give you a clear field. If I do that, there's nothing to stop you."

"Christ, Floraine, you got to give me time—" The unfinished sentence was punctuated by a sharply indrawn breath.

"What's the matter?" she whispered.

I thought he had heard my breathing, and I raised my gun and waited. But it wasn't me that had taken the wind out of his words. None of the three of us had heard the front door open or anyone come in. But the door had opened and someone had come in. It was Kerch's voice I heard next, speaking from the direction of the hallway:

"I sent Garland to bring you in, Sault. What a charming excuse you have for not having come. You might as well frisk him, Garland, though I suspect he hasn't the courage to carry a gun. Please don't feel that it's necessary to cover your breasts, my dear Floraine. Garland isn't interested, Rusty won't molest you so long as I'm here, and the sight of them continues to give me a certain aesthetic pleasure."

She said one word: "Toad!"

"You women," Kerch said pleasantly. "You women are always eager to be deluded by such nonessentials as personal beauty. Joe's here, for example. He's quite a nice-looking youngster, but he's got the heart of a little slinking rat. Isn't that right, Joey?"

Joey said: "Floraine—Mrs. Weather here—just called me up down at Malteoni's, and I came over here to see what was bothering her. We just kind of got playing around, you know how it is—"

"Toads are hard to kill," Kerch said sententiously. "He's not carrying anything, is he, Garland?"

"No. John Weather took his knife off him before he left town."

"See what a frail reed you've been leading on, Floraine? I really can't commend your choice of partners."

"He doesn't look like a toad," she said.

"As I do, of course? But then you didn't choose me as a partner. I chose you. At any rate, there are uglier things than toads. I predict that when we've finished with Joey, he won't be able to compete even with me in loveliness."

"I wasn't going to do it," Joey said in a hushed voice. "I was just pumping her so I could give you the word. Christ, I wouldn't try anything on you, Mr. Kerch, we always got along great!"

"That seems to be finished, doesn't it, Joey? Quite as finished as you will shortly be. Help him to stand up, Rusty. I think we'll go out to the Wildwood."

"Take your hands off me," Joey yelled. "You do anything to me and I'll tear your setup wide open."

"I don't know what you mean, Joey."

"You know what I mean. I know enough to pin murder on you, Kerch. If they can't get you for murder, they can get you for accessory."

"I always knew you killed Jerry Weather," Floraine said. "Now I've got something on you, Kerch."

"Nobody's got anything on me at all," Kerch said. "Bring him along, Rusty. We want to get out to the Wildwood before it's light."

"If you do anything to me, I'll sing," Sault said.

I saw him led, struggling feebly, across the narrow section of the room that was visible through the crack. Rusty had his arm and Garland walked behind him in a death march.

"You won't sing," Kerch said, "if what we do to you shuts you up for good. Come along, Floraine. You'll need a coat."

"You can't do without me," she said. "You're crazy if you think you can."

"Perfectly true, my dear. I can't do without you. But I can certainly do without Joey Sault. Come along."

Chapter 13

I stood where I was while Floraine got her coat and Kerch turned out the light in the front room. The front door closed behind them, and their footsteps receded on the walk. Kerch had been the last to leave, and I had missed my chance to shoot him. The thought of shooting him then hadn't even occurred to me. New questions were rising in my mind like bubbles in a stirred drink, and the death of Kerch wouldn't answer any of them. Besides, Floraine wanted him dead, which gave me a reason for wanting him kept alive. For a while, listening to Sault and Floraine, I had begun to believe that Floraine had killed my father and that Kerch knew of it, but what she and Sault said at the end made me doubt it again. Suspicion wavered but continually swung back to Kerch, like a compass needle to the north.

If only I could get Kerch alone, I thought as I pulled on my boots. Such smooth talkers were nearly always gnawed by internal weaknesses and fears. And I remembered what Carla had said about him. As soft as jelly. If I could get my hands on him. My bootlace broke, and I swore at it and tied it in the dark at the top of the stairs.

I remembered vaguely where the Wildwood was; it was a roadhouse that my father had owned, six or seven miles north of the city. Too far to walk, and it might be dangerous to take a cab. But Floraine should have a car.

I went down the hall to the master bedroom which my mother had shared with my father before she left him. When I turned on the light I saw that it was Floraine's now. Frilled curtains at the windows, mules under the chenille-covered bed, which I noticed hadn't been slept in, a dressing-table with a triple mirror, a heavy odor of perfume, which grew heavier when I approached the dressing-table. There was a Corde purse on it, thrown carelessly among an array of bottles and jars. I unzipped the purse and found her car keys where I had hoped they'd be.

Just before I turned out the light, a picture on the wall above the bed caught my eye. It was a still life, crowded with brilliantly colored tropical flowers. My heart beat once and the picture wasn't a still life after all, and the flowers weren't flowers. They were hands and faces and other parts of human bodies, male and female. Another heartbeat, and they were flowers again. I turned out the light and left the house, thinking that my father's last sexual fling had carried him a hell of a long way—a hell of a long way down.

The keys fitted the Packard roadster that I found in the garage. I backed it out slowly and headed north at a speed that wouldn't be worth a policeman's second glance. About five miles out of town I came to a gas station that contained a light and a man moving in front of it. I turned in and parked by the pumps. I didn't need gas, but he'd be able to tell me exactly where the Wildwood was. I didn't want to get there before I expected to.

A thin man in grease-stained dungarees came out of the station yawning, his face still caked with sleep.

"You want gas?"

"Not just now. Maybe you can tell me where the Wildwood is?"

"Yeah, but somebody gave you the wrong dope, brother. It's been closed up since gas-rationing, and ain't never been opened yet. I wish to hell they'd open it again—it used to make business for me."

"A friend of mine told me he lives out past there. We're going fishing."

"What's his name?"

"Piscator," I said. "Peter Piscator."

"Funny, I thought I knew everybody that lives out

in that direction. But I never heard of this guy Piscator."

"He's a recluse. Now where's the Wildwood?"

"Second road to your left. Go down a mile and
you'll see it on the right-hand side. I hope you find
your friend O.K. If you don't, come back here and I'll
see if I can find him in the phone book." He was
treating me with the respect my Packard deserved, but
I'd have preferred a car that was less easily remembered.

I thanked him and drove away. When I left the concrete at the second turning to the left, I drove even
more slowly than before, with my eyes straining ahead
past the white fan of the headlights. It was a gravel
road with woods on both sides, and completely deserted. It was too late even for parking couples. I could
see Kerch's point in taking Sault to this godforsaken
neck of the woods. I switched off the lights and drove
by the faint light of the stars.

My mileage had increased six tenths of a mile since
leaving the main road when I came to a dirt lane leading into the woods. I went up it a hundred yards or so,
past the first turning, and parked in the ditch after turning the car around. A weather-beaten sign nailed to a
tree said: "Five Hundred yards to Wildwood Inn—
Steaks and Cocktails—Never a Cover Charge."

After a quarter of a mile of cautious walking in the
ditch I saw ahead of me a black car parked under a
tree against the fence. I took out my gun and approached it as noiselessly as I could. I didn't need the
gun: the car was empty. The engine was warm, though,
and it looked like the car I had seen Garland driving
on Fenton Boulevard.

I had scarcely left it when I saw a dim yellow light
shining through the trees on the right side of the road. I
slipped through the wire fence and circled the light,
staying in the cover of the woods. It was light, second-
growth timber, easy to make my way through, and the
damp spring earth muffled my footfalls. My eyes were
becoming adjusted to darkness, and I could make out
the main outlines of the building I was circling, a long,

low building with its length parallel to the road, fronted
by a gravel square for drive-ins. A short wing sur-
mounted by a wide chimney jutted out the back at the
rear end, and that was where the light was coming
from. A shadow moved across the cracked, yellow
blind, and I thought I recognized the shape of Kerch's
shapeless body.

I cut deeper into the woods and, walking a little less
cautiously, widened my circle to the rear. Finally I
came out in a clearing where there were several piles of
cordwood. A path led from there to the back of the
inn, probably to the kitchen. I followed it till I saw the
light again, shining through an unblinded window at
the back. My right hand hugged the butt of my gun,
and my thumb took off the safety almost by instinct.

The howl that a coyote raises to the moon can be
disturbing, but it's a mindless lamentation, which really
bothers only the superstitious. The scream of a hurt cat
is ugly too, but it doesn't echo long in the emotions.
There are a lot of cats, and they do a lot of yelling, and
one of them is always getting hurt. Of course, there are
a lot of men, more than two billion of them, and one of
them dies every second, or whatever the figure is. I had
seen a hundred corpses lying in a field at once, and another hundred half-gone and making a noise about it.
Still, when a man screams in agony, it shakes more
than the eardrums.

I was at the window before the scream ended, careless about whether I'd be seen or not. The screams had
divided the night into two countries, with a deep gulf
between. I was on the side of the man who was being
hurt, and the people who were hurting him were on the
other.

Joe Sault was in a kitchen chair half-facing me, with
Kerch in front of him and Rusty behind him holding
his arms. His left ear hung down like a red rag, drip-
ping blood rhythmically onto his stylish collar. His
mouth was ragged and spongy. His body was naked
from the waist down, and his shirt had been rolled up
under his armpits. His lean belly, bisected by a line of

dark hair, trembled steadily like a beaten dog's. His genitals were blue and shrunken with fright.

Floraine was sitting with her fur-coated back to me, almost against the window. She didn't move and she didn't say a word. Garland was standing beside her, but all I could see of him was the gray elbow of his coat. The vibrating white light of a gasoline lamp on the table gave the room an ugliness as precise as a raw photograph.

Kerch put down the heavy iron spoon that he had been balancing in his hand, and picked up a paring knife from the table. Before he began to move, I sensed that he was going to turn, and ducked out of sight.

"You're insane," she said—"insane with vanity and jealousy."

"Not at all, my dear. The regrets with which I look back to the handsome days of my youth are thoroughly wistful and mild, I assure you. And surely I couldn't be jealous of an aging slut like yourself, could I?"

"You're eaten up with jealousy," she said. "Did you ever imagine I took pleasure in having a diseased thing like you crawl into my bed? Why do you think I left you in the first place?"

"You're singing a new song, my dear. You have quite a repertory."

"Toad!"

"You've become insolent, lately, haven't you? You need a stern lesson, Floraine. Now take this knife and do what I tell you."

"Toad!"

"I've tried to be agreeable to you for nearly two years. You can expect much more severe disciplining in the future."

"Toad!"

"Don't call me that." His voice had risen gradually to a high, thin monotone. There was the sound of a blow on flesh. The woman gasped.

"All right," she said dully. "Give me the knife."

When she stood up I could see her red, tangled hair and broad shoulders. Sault uttered a loud groan, modulated by the half-formed syllables of words. Floraine's right shoulder leaned forward slightly as she took the knife. Over her left shoulder I could see part of Kerch's face. I saw him smile for the first and last time. It was a wide, toothy smile, like a shark's, rendered unique by the tip of tongue that protruded between the teeth.

Her right hand holding the small, bright knife rose suddenly above her shoulder and descended into Kerch's smile. A thin red line appeared in the cheek below the heavy right eye and widened. Kerch yelped, sprawled backwards across Sault's bare knees, and rolled heavily onto the floor. Garland stepped between Floraine and the window, and pinned her arms behind her.

Kerch crawled across the floor and stood up with the knife in his hand. Half of his face was shining with blood. He eyes were unfocused, as dull as brown eggs. I couldn't see Floraine's face, but I could see the vigorous movements of his right arm and shoulder up and down, back and forth, as he worked on it with the knife. When I got back to my car a quarter of a mile away, I could still hear her screams—or thought I could.

Chapter 14

"Couldn't find him, eh?" the man in dungarees said when I stopped the car. "What's the matter, friend? You look worried."

"I couldn't find the house. I'm not what you'd call worried, but I'd like to get out there before he leaves. Can I use your phone?"

"Yeah, but I looked it up and he ain't in the phone book. Spell it 'P-i-s,' don't you?"

"That's right. I want to call another fellow that knows him."

"If he lives in the city, it costs a dime to phone the city."

I changed a ten and gave him a quarter. He pointed out the phone on the wall of his tiny office. "That's the phone book there on the table."

"Do you mind stepping out and closing the door?" I said. "This is a private call."

He looked at me suspiciously. "You ain't going to make a long-distance call? You can't make no long-distance calls on this phone."

I tossed him another quarter. "Go away for a minute, will you? I'm calling the city and I'm in a hurry."

"O.K., friend. Long as it ain't no long-distance call." He walked out slowly, in token of his right to remain where he was, and slammed the door behind him.

I riffled through the first pages of the phone book and found the Al's. Allbright. Allen. Allin. Allison. If Kerch and the other four in the Wildwood could be caught as they were, literally red-handed, the rotten core of the city would be smashed wide open. It had to be done now, before Floraine and Sault were silenced for good. But Kerch had two gunmen and I knew that,

117

single-handed, I wouldn't be able to take the five of them alive. Yet I couldn't call the police. Allister was the only one I could count on.

Allister's name wasn't in the phone book. That meant he had a privately listed number! The City Hall? No, there wouldn't be anybody there at this time. I called the operator and told her I had to talk to the Mayor. She told me she couldn't give me his number, and cut me off with a lilting "Sorry."

It looked as if I'd have to drive back to town. But that might give the people at the Wildwood time to clean up and get away. And if the city police picked me up driving a stolen car, it would be the end of everything—the end of me. I had a last chance, the number which Allister had called from his house when he got me the gun. I remembered it as well as the date I was released from the army—23748.

I asked for the number and chewed the inside of my lower lip while the phone at the other end of the line rang four times. A woman's sleepy voice said: "Hello?"

I thought it was a voice I had heard before, but I was never good at recognizing voices over the telephone. "I have a message for Mayor Allister—"

"Call his house, why don't you?" the woman said petulantly. "He's at home, isn't he?"

"I can't get his number. Can you give it to me?"

"How am I supposed to know? I don't know the Mayor. You've got your gall calling me in the middle of the night—"

"Don't hang up," I said quickly. "Listen to me. This is dead serious. Will you deliver a message to Allister?"

"Who are you, anyway?" the woman whined.

"I'm a friend of his. I need his help. Will you please give him a message?"

"What's the message? Depends on what it is."

"This is it. Come to the Wildwood Inn now. If you have any honest police, bring them. If not, bring a posse of citizens. There's a murder going on."

"What?"

I repeated the message. "Have you got that? Allister's got to get it immediately."

"Yeah. Yeah, I got it." Her voice had been scraped bare of sleepiness. "Who shall I tell him sent it?"

"John," I said. "He'll know. You'll tell him right away?"

"Get off the wire and give me a chance."

I hung up.

"You find out O.K.?" the thin man said, as I climbed into the roadster.

"Yeah. Thanks very much."

"You're welcome. You know how it is about those long-distance calls."

"Yeah." I used every ounce of pickup the car had as I turned up the highway.

I found the lane and parked in the same place, leaving the motor idling. Instead of going back to the gravel road, I cut straight through the woods. The blue steel concavity of the sky was whitening at the edges, giving me enough light to see by. Before I reached the Wildwood it was chilly aluminum dawn.

The front of the inn, faced with roughhewn logs, had a certain rustic charm, especially at night. In the morning light its back kitchen looked like the underside of appearances, the pocked hindquarters of reality. Leprous yellow paint, blistered by summer and cracked by winter, peeled from the weather-warped boards. The broken steps to the back door were flanked by a row of rusting garbage pails, half of them overturned. At the end of the row there was a six-foot pile of empty cans and bottles, like a sardonic pyramid to a tinhorn Pharaoh.

While I watched from the trees beside the path, the back door opened and Rusty Jahnke came out carrying a spade over his shoulder. He set it against the wall, took off his topcoat, rolled it up, and left it on the stoop. Then he tested the bare earth with his spade in several places. Finally he found a soft spot beside the pile of cans, and began to dig.

He worked fast, breathing audibly through his nose, and the pattern of his excavation took shape. It was about six feet long and three feet wide. When it was a little more than a foot deep, he quit digging, leaned momentarily on his spade, and took off his suit coat. He folded it and put it on top of the other. But when he began digging again, his shoulder holster got in his way. He unsnapped the harness and took it off, laying it down carefully on the stoop.

He began working again, harder than before, and a dark blotch of sweat appeared on his shirt and spread gradually across his back. It looked like the best chance I'd ever have to put him out of action.

I stepped into the path and walked towards him. When the muzzle of my gun was four feet from his bent spine, I said: "Raise your hands. Don't speak. Don't move."

His hands jerked above his head and the spade stayed where it was, upright in the earth. I clubbed the gun, took a long step forward, and swung it by the muzzle against the base of his skull. It made a sharp cracking sound like an axe on wood. He lay down quietly in the shallow grave he had dug.

I tossed the gun, caught it by the butt, and turned towards the closed door of the kitchen. There was no sound, no movement, as if all life had ceased with my single blow. I took a step towards the door, another, and another. The tarnished brass knob turned and the door sprang open. I fired twice through the center of the opening, then saw that there was nothing there to hit. Three long steps brought me under the window, where I crouched against the wall watching the door. The window flew up with a snap above my head. I wasted two more bullets through the open window. That left me two, or was it three? I couldn't risk reloading. I was beginning to get frightened, and it made me a little trigger-happy.

I saw the shoulder of a gray coat edging around the corner of the door. I emptied my gun into it and saw the triangle of black holes appear in the cloth. Then the coat collapsed and fell across the doorsill. It was empty. I had used all seven bullets to drill air.

The gun in Rusty's holster was a forlorn chance, but I jumped for it and got my hand on the butt. The harness was wrapped around it and the gun got tangled in the straps. I wrenched at them, infuriated by the animistic feeling that doors, windows, guns—all physical objects—were conspiring with Kerch against me.

"Drop it," Garland said from the doorway. "I'm getting pretty tired of you."

I hesitated a moment, holding the useless gun. He fired once and it flew out of my hand, leaving it numb. I looked at him and saw that he had done it from the hip. I could feel my nerve draining out of me like water.

"You should know by now that I mean what I say." He tripped down the steps and walked around me. "Go inside. Take it slow. I'll kill you for any reason at all."

I climbed the steps on shaky legs and stepped inside the kitchen. My foot slipped on the floor and I almost fell.

"Take it easy," Garland said. "You almost got it that time. I can put a line of slugs right up your backbone like a punch machine."

"I know you're good," I said. "You don't have to keep telling me."

"No more cracks out of you, fellow," he said from behind me. "I didn't kill you, because Kerch might want to see you alive. But I can always change my mind. Or drill your fanny for you."

I didn't make the obvious retort. My throat was busy resisting the fierce pressure of nausea that clenched my stomach and squirted streams of saliva into my mouth. It may have been the slick of blood on the floor where my foot had slipped. It may have been the half-naked man in the corner with the discolored neck and dead, swollen face. It may have been the woman who lay on the table with her limp legs dangling over the end. The gasoline lamp had been moved to the stove and shone fully on the bloody towel which wrapped her face. The rhythmic bubbling sounds of her breathing were the only sign that she was still alive.

"Pretty, isn't it?" Garland said. "You see what happens to boys and girls that try to buck our organization."

I had conquered the nausea, but the effort had left

me weak. I sat down with my back to the window. The soles of my boots were sticky when I moved my feet. Garland sat down facing me in the chair where Sault had died. He held the gun politely on his knee, like a cup of tea. I began to estimate the minimum time it would take for Allister to come with help. If everything went well, it seemed to me that he could get there any minute.

"You're very foolish to come back, fellow," Garland said. "Kerch isn't going to like it a little bit."

I looked at him, and didn't answer. His slender fingers, delicate features, girlish mouth, made a strange contrast with the pleasure he took in killing. His gray eyes held no history. I couldn't imagine behind him a boyhood of school, family life, ambition, or any kind of hope. He looked as if he had been always what he was, as if he had emerged from the womb murderous, cheaply elegant, and epicene.

"While we're waiting," he said after a while, "you might as well bring Rusty in. He'll catch cold out there."

"That would be a terrible pity."

"Get going," he snapped. "You go first now. Remember I can drop a man with this gun up to fifty yards."

Rusty was lying where he had fallen in the raw earth, his arms outspread and his face turned awkwardly to one side. His knees were drawn up slightly, and, though his eyes were open, the lower rims of the pupils were barely visible under the lids.

Without taking his eyes or gun from me, Garland crouched and felt the great swelling under the red hair. "You hit him a nasty smack," he said indifferently. "It's a good thing Salamander's coming."

"Salamander?" I remembered the dried-up little man in the radio station who claimed to be the seventh son of a seventh son.

"He used to be a doctor," Garland said in a gossipy way. "He lost his license when they sent him up. Now, pick Rusty up and be careful not to drop him." He giggled. "Or I'll drop *you* right in your tracks, fellow."

Rusty was hard to handle, because his back was rigid and his bent legs refused to straighten, but I finally got him over my shoulder and up the steps into the kitchen. I laid him on the floor beside the dead man.

"They make a pretty pair, don't they?" Garland said. "Now go and sit down and be thankful there aren't three of you on the floor."

"Aren't you going to do anything for this woman?"

"We did what we could. I wasn't the one that cut her. If you ask me, it was a bad mistake. She's still breathing, isn't she?"

"Yes, but she's losing blood."

"Salamander should be here soon. I'm no doctor."

After a pause, during which I sat and looked at his gun some more, he said: "Maybe you better finish that hole Rusty started. Kerch won't like it if Sault's still above ground."

"Kerch won't like it if anybody's still above ground."

"Maybe you're right, fellow." He smiled a sad little smile, and stood up again. "Walk ahead of me. You might as well dig it deep enough for two."

I was sweating and digging with blistered hands, shoulder-deep in the grave, when the sound of the car came down the road and stopped in front of the inn. My first thought was that Allister had come, and I stopped digging and straightened up.

"Go on digging," Garland said above me. "You want to make a good impression on Mr. Kerch, don't you?"

Kerch came around the corner of the building, followed by the man who called himself Professor Salamander. There was a long gauze bandage on the side of Kerch's face, held in place by strips of adhesive. He looked as worried and excited as his wide phlegmatic face could ever look.

"What's this, Garland?" he said when he saw me.

"Boy friend here came along and hurt Rusty, so I put him to work. I told him to dig it deep enough for two, didn't I, boy friend?"

"You're very audacious," Kerch said to me. "Your audacity will be the death of you."

"Electricity will be the death of you. I think you'll all die in a chair before long."

"Keep him digging," Kerch said to Garland. "Don't shoot him unless you have to. I may have another use for him."

"Where's the injured lady?" Salamander said in his rich voice.

"In the kitchen."

They went in and closed the door.

I went on digging in a slowing rhythm. I was very tired. The blood beat painfully in my sore head. Some of the blisters had broken, leaving my hands raw. The hole was up to my chin when I straightened up.

"That should be deep enough," Garland said. "It's probably only temporary anyway."

"Do I climb out now, or do I just stay here?"

"You can come in and get Sault and fill it up."

I was so tired that I didn't realize for a minute what that meant. It meant that I wasn't going to share the grave with Sault.

In the kitchen, the ex-doctor was working over Floraine Weather's ex-face. I looked once, and looked away. Kerch's vanity had been thoroughly avenged. The only human thing left about the woman was the little bubbling sound her breath still made.

"I can't save her," Salamander said. "She's lost too much blood."

"She has to be kept alive," Kerch said from where he sat at the window. "If you don't save her, you'll do no more abortions in this town. I could have you put away for the rest of your life, Professor."

The old man looked at Kerch with panic in his little, yellow eyes. "I tell you I can't save her. The only thing that would save her is a transfusion. She's in profound shock."

"Then give her a transfusion." Kerch glanced at me. "Here's a healthy young source of blood for you."

"I can't! I haven't got the instruments. I don't know what her blood type is. If you want to save her, you've got to take her to a hospital. Even then, it's probably too late."

"No, we can't do that," Kerch said slowly. "How long will it take her to die?"

"She might live for a couple of hours. I can't give you an accurate estimate. She's not losing any more blood."

"Take out the stitches, then. If she has to die, she had better die quickly. I can't wait a couple of hours."

Salamander looked at him in horror. "Take out the stitches?"

"That is what I said. Then you can attend to Rusty. What do you want, Garland?"

"The hole's about five feet deep. Is that deep enough?"

"I think so," Kerch said. "We'll make other arrangements later, when we're not so pressed for time."

"Pick him up, fellow," Garland said to me. "Pick him up and bring him along."

Death had not yet stiffened Sault's body, but he wasn't convenient to carry. Perhaps it was simply that I had never buried a man before, and it made me weak. I carried him gently, but the final drop into the earth jarred a gasp of air out of his lungs. I covered his body with earth before I covered his upturned face. It was hard to throw the spadeful that hid his dead face from the sky.

Garland recited a derisive singsong:

"Ashes to ashes,
Dust to dust:
If God don't get you,
The Devil must."

"I thought he was a friend of yours."

"Nobody is a friend of mine," he said seriously. "What do you think I am, a softie?"

Before I had finished filling the grave, Kerch opened the door and called to Garland: "Bring him in here."

"Quick march," Garland said.

They had wrapped the woman in a car rug, head and all. Kerch ordered me to carry her out and put her in the back seat of the car. I did this. Already I was getting the mortuary feeling that dead bodies weren't human any more, merely clumsy bundles to be disposed of. The woman wouldn't have been comfortable with her head in the corner of the seat and her swathed legs twisted sideways onto the floor, but her comfort no longer mattered.

When Garland and I returned to the kitchen, Kerch ripped a button from my coat and a few hairs from my head. Garland's gun in the small of my back kept me from taking hold of him.

"Now let me see," Kerch said. "It would be nice if he carried a knife."

Garland dipped his free hand in my pocket and brought out the spring knife. "But this is Sault's," he said.

"All the better," Kerch said. "The more confusion, the better."

He dropped the knife in his pocket and put my button and hair in an envelope. "You stay here, Garland, and take care of Weather. The Professor says that Rusty will come around if we just leave him. I should be back in two or three hours. If anyone interferes with you in the meantime, I'll probably be at Alonzo Sanford's house."

"Can I shoot him if he acts too wise?" Garland said.

"It would be more convenient if you didn't, not just now. But use your own judgment. Come along, Professor."

The little man scampered after him like a frightened lizard. Their motor roared, receded, and faded out in the distance. I had given up hope of Allister, who had either failed to get my message or disregarded it, but a new hope formed in my tired muscles and rose to my head. Garland was a terrifying shot, but otherwise he wasn't much of a man, and he was the only one I had to deal with. If I could get close enough to touch him before Kerch returned, before Rusty came to, before his bullet could find me. I closed my eyes so he couldn't see them, and sat thinking in the dark.

"Be very careful," he said, as if he could read my mind. "I've got this gun on you all the time."

I didn't open my eyes or answer him. After a while I heard the click of his lighter and the tiny crackling of a cigarette taking fire, and a few minutes later the light plop of the butt on the floor and the grinding of his heel as he put it out. The gasoline lamp hissed constantly like a simmering kettle on the stove.

Much later, I heard the scrape of his chair as he got up. My head was tilted back, and I scarcely had to raise my eyelids to see him. He was walking sideways towards the sink, watching me from the corners of his eyes. Shifting the gun to his left hand, he turned on the tap, rinsed a clouded tumbler which he took from a shelf above the sink, and filled it with water. When the lower rim of the tilted glass was in his mouth and the upper rim was approaching the bridge of his nose, I moved.

He fired twice before I reached him, but the bullets went over my crouched back. Then my shoulder caught him in the belly and bore him backwards against the sink. My right hand found the gun and took it away from him. I clenched my fingers in his fair, waved hair and beat his head against the edge of the sink until he no longer struggled. Then I took each of his slender wrists in turn, and snapped it across my knee. I was getting pretty tired of Garland.

Chapter 15

The Packard was waiting where I left it, with the engine still running. The tank was less than half full, but that was more than enough to take me where I wanted to go. I drove back to the concrete highway but left it at the first turning, in order to avoid my inquisitive friend at the gas station, and entered the city by another road. It was too early for the residents of the north side to be going to work, but even there I saw signs that the city was waking up. There were lights in many of the houses and some traffic on the streets. I passed a garbage truck and a milk truck, a man in overalls rolling a lawn-mower along the sidewalk, a few colored girls coming up from the black ghetto on the other side of Lillian Street to wash the glasses from last night's parties and give their white mistresses breakfast in bed.

Before I reached Sanford's house, a cruising police car came up behind me and slid slowly by. I had an impulse to stop my car and duck down in the seat, but the patrol car went on and paid no attention to me. The sudden pounding of my heart and my white-knuckled grip on the wheel told me what a chance I was taking, but I had no alternative—unless I wanted to leave town and drop the case just when it seemed to be breaking. I didn't want to do that. No, I did want to do it, but I couldn't.

I circled the block in which Sanford's house stood alone. I couldn't see any trace of Kerch's black car, but there were lights on in the house, upstairs and down. I parked in the side street by the tennis courts, and walked up the back driveway to the service entrance at the rear of the house.

The Negro maid who had let me in the night before was washing dishes at an open window beside the door. Her profile was to me, and I could see her lips moving as she talked steadily to herself:

"Keep me up till all hours and then get me up in the middle of the night to make breakfast six o'clock in the morning. Who they think I am, the mechanical girl they showed down in the window of the five-and-ten? Fetch and carry, bring me a drink, just bring me the *yolks* of three eggs. I can't eat the white, what's the matter with you, girl, this toast is like it's made out of old leather? Yes, Mr. Sanford, no Mr. Sanford—Mr. Sanford, kiss my rump."

She threw down a final spoon with a clatter, and dumped the dishpan in the sink. Throwing back her head in a buoyant gesture, which contrasted with her growling voice, she began to sing the opening bars of *I Wanna Get Married*. Her eyes roved around and saw me at the door, and she stopped in the middle of the line. I knocked tactfully as if I had just arrived, and she opened the door, talking:

"Ain't nothing for you to do today, and the cook got orders from Mr. Sanford not to feed anybody at all at the door. Wait a minute, though, if you want to wait around for a while until Sim gets up, he might let you polish one of the cars, he was saying yesterday the Lincoln needed washing, if you want to wait."

"I'm not looking for work." I took a dollar out of my wallet and wrapped the end of it around my forefinger.

"Say, ain't you the man that was here last night? What you doing, coming to the back door? You want to see Mr. Sanford again?"

"Is he up?"

"Yeah, but I don't think he wants to see anybody this early in the morning. Wait a minute, I'll go and see. You can come in here if you don't want to go around to the front. Say, your clothes is a mess. What's the matter with you, mister?"

She opened the door and I slipped her the dollar. "I was in an accident."

"You wait here. I'll go and ask—"

"No, don't disturb Mr. Sanford. I'm looking for a man called Kerch. Do you know him?"

"I ought to. He had breakfast with Mr. Sanford this morning." She relapsed into her singsong monologue: "Get up at six o'clock and make breakfast for two people because the cook isn't here yet. I wasn't hired for a cook."

"Listen to me. Is Kerch still here?"

"No, he left. Four fried eggs I had to give him. Six slices of toast he ate. Juice of five oranges. And he didn't even have the manners to leave me anything." She caught herself up and looked at me a little nervously. "Mr. Kerch a friend of yours?"

"Has Mr. Kerch got any friends?"

She allowed her lips to stretch in a large, warm smile. "Not likely. Mr. Sanford is a friend of his, though, I guess."

"If you served them breakfast, you probably heard what they were talking about."

Her dark face stiffened and she gave me a narrow look. "I never talk about anything that goes on in the front of the house. Mr. Sanford's strict with us about that, and don't you forget he could fix me so I'd never get another job in this town."

I took a ten out of my wallet, folded it carefully, and tucked it in the frilled pocket of her apron. She made a token gesture of repelling the contamination, but she let the bill stay in the pocket.

"I'm not asking you to give away any secrets," I said. "I think I know what they were talking about. All I want is confirmation."

She smiled again. "You give me ten dollars so you can tell me what Mr. Sanford was talking about at breakfast?"

"I'll tell you, then you tell me whether I'm right."

"All right, mister. I'm listening."

"They were talking about the property of a woman called Mrs. Weather."

"They didn't say nothing about no Mrs. Weather—"

"Floraine, then. Did they mention Floraine?"

"Go on, mister. I'm still listening."

"Kerch was in a hurry to sell Floraine's property to Mr. Sanford. Am I warm?"

"You're hot, mister. You're burning up. How you know all this?"

"I'm a good guesser. But there's one thing I can't guess. Was Mr. Sanford willing to buy? Did the deal go through?"

"I don't know," the maid said. "Mr. Sanford told me to take the trays out and not come back. But I don't think he wanted to do it. He had that frozen-face look, *you* know."

"Yeah," I said. "I've seen it. Where's Mr. Sanford now?"

"He's still up in his room, I guess. He reads all the time in the morning before he goes over to the office. I never saw a man read so much."

"Go and ask him if he'll see me, will you?"

"Yes, sir. I'll ask him." But she lingered in the kitchen and finally said: "You won't tell him I was talking to you about Mr. Kerch? That'd be my job for sure."

"I won't tell him," I promised. "I appreciate your help."

"I appreciate your eleven bucks." She flashed me another smile. "Maybe you better come in the front hall and wait. The cook'll be here any time and she don't like people in the kitchen."

I waited in the hall while she danced up the baronial staircase and a minute later danced down:

"Mr. Sanford says you can come right up. It's the door that's open at the top of the stairs."

He was sitting by a tall window in a leather armchair, which emphasized by its amplitude the thinness of his shrunken body. His silk robe fostered the illusion, supported by his changeless pallor and the unsleeping vigilance of his cold eyes, that he had been up all night. But the wide, Elizabethan bed in the alcove behind him was unmade.

He turned his book over on his knee—it was the Everyman's edition of *Progress and Poverty*—and looked up at me: "You'll excuse my not getting up."

I sat down in the armchair facing him. "You'll excuse my sitting down. I've been running around all night trying to clean up your lousy town. It's tiring."

"You look tired," he said drily. "You seem, too, to have gotten yourself rather thoroughly mussed in the course of your nocturnal crusade."

I cut in harshly on his careful urbanity: "I came here to warn you, Mr. Sanford. Kerch left me an hour or two ago, and I heard he was on his way to see you. Does he, by any chance, have Floraine Weather's power of attorney?"

He took off his reading glasses and looked at me. A kind of smile puckered the flesh around his eyes and fanned the crow's-feet almost back to his ears. "That's a somewhat interrogative warning, is it not?"

"The warning will come in a minute. You might as well answer my question. I can easily find out anyway."

He didn't say anything for a while. He folded his glasses and tapped them on the withered knuckles of his left hand. "As a matter of fact, he does. He's Mrs. Weather's business agent, you know."

"And he negotiated the sale of the hotel to you?"

"He did. It was Mrs. Weather's wish, and he acted for her. You'd be foolish to think it wasn't a perfectly legitimate proposition."

"Of course, Kerch wouldn't offer you a proposition that wasn't perfectly legitimate. And naturally, if he did, you wouldn't wish to have anything to do with it. That's why I'm warning you."

"But against what eventuality are you warning me? Your warnings are excessively cryptic, aren't they?"

"Did Kerch try to sell you the rest of my father's property?—the Cathay Club and the radio station?"

"If he had, it would not have been any concern of yours. I repeat, if he had."

"Who administered my father's estate?"

"The County National Bank. But why you should choose me to instruct you in your family's affairs—"

"I'm doing you a favor. I'm keeping the holy name of Sanford out of a very nasty criminal case. The County National's your bank, isn't it?"

The old man sighed. His breath rustled through the passages of his head like a desert wind in a dying tree. "People who know nothing of the intricacies of a financial structure—people like yourself—might call it mine. I'm chairman of the board."

"You told me last night I was Mrs. Weather's heir. Is that the straight dope?"

"I'm not sure I understand your jargon—"

"You can't snub me," I said unpleasantly. "You didn't get where you are by talking with six-syllable words at pink-tea parties. Were you telling me the truth?"

He made a weary gesture with his hand. "Why should I tell you anything but the truth? The will was probated long ago."

"Then the sale of my father's property is very much my concern. I own it."

"Aren't you rather anticipating events? Mrs. Weather is the owner. She has given Mr. Kerch the legal right to act for her in all her business arrangements. I hope that's clear."

"It's clear but it's not true. Floraine Weather died a couple of hours ago."

His keen, pale eyes probed my face and looked away again. "I don't know whether to believe you. What did she die of, if she died?"

"You'll read it in the papers. I only came here to warn you. Don't try to buy anything that belonged to my father, or you'll get into very bad trouble. Maybe you're in it already."

"I'm inclined to doubt it." He spoke evenly, but he was leaning forward in his chair. "I may as well tell you that I wouldn't touch Kerch's proposition. It struck me as much too hasty. As a matter of fact, I was determined to talk it over with Mrs. Weather." He raised his left hand a few inches and dropped it back on the arm of his chair. "Now you tell me she's dead."

"But you bought the hotel."

"Why should I not?"

"It's possible that neither Floraine Weather nor her agent had any right to sell it. A murderer can't inherit property from his victim, isn't that the law?"

"I don't believe there's a law on the subject." He smiled slightly. "But it's something that isn't done. The principle has the status of an unwritten law in our courts. You're not suggesting that your stepmother murdered your father? She had, you know, what they call a perfect alibi."

"No doubt she had. That wouldn't prevent her from conspiring to murder him."

"Conspiring with whom?"

"That's what I'm trying to find out." I rose to go.

"Just a minute, John," the old man said. "If what you tell me is true, and I assume it is, you're in the position of stepping into your father's shoes, so to speak."

"Not literally," I said. "He died in them."

"You understand me, I think. Your father enjoyed a unique position in this city, John. I think I can say he and I established an efficient, and quite profitable, system of co-operation between our various interests. Perhaps, if you'll consider the situation for a few days, I'm certain you'll come to the conclusion that co-operation is a desirable thing. Particularly in a middle-sized community like ours—"

"I understand you, all right. Now that I've come into a little property you think I'm worth buying."

He wagged his white hand under his nose. "Nothing was further from my thoughts. But I don't see why we can't be friends. Your father and I were close friends over a period of many years. Come and see me in a few days, John. I think you're somewhat shaken emotionally, this morning."

"Murder always leaves me emotionally shaken."

"Murder? What murder? Was Mrs. Weather murdered?"

I left him with the questions echoing unanswered in his dry old ears.

Chapter 16

Floraine Weather lived, when she was alive, only a few blocks from Sanford's house. I drove there with the idea that I'd probably find her at home. Parking her car around the corner, I went on foot to her front door. A maid who was sweeping the steps of the house next door, the one on the corner, glanced at me as I climbed the porch, so I went through the motions of ringing the bell. After waiting a minute I tried the door, found it open, and went in.

The curtains in the front room were still drawn, but enough light came through them to show what was in the room. She was lying by the chesterfield on which she had tried, the night before, to persuade Joey Sault to let greatness be thrust upon him. Her body had been arranged in a grotesque and awkward position, half-leaning against the chesterfield with her legs sprawled wide and her chin on her shoulder. In the subdued light of the quiet, beautiful room, it was as if a corpse laid out in a funeral parlor had, in a last bitter spasm of life, viciously parodied the final peace of the dead.

I moved into the center of the room and looked down at her. The knife that I had taken from Sault lay open and blood-smeared on the rug beside her twisted leg. Above the grimy mask of congealed blood which disguised her throat and the lower part of her face, her open eyes regarded me steadfastly. I didn't want to do it, but I kneeled beside her and looked at her hands. Between the fingers of one I found the hair that Kerch had plucked from my head, and I took it back. The button from my coat had been placed under her body, and I had to move her before I found it. She was stiffer and colder than she had been, all but returned to the resistant mindlessness of inanimate objects. Kerch was giving me lessons in the natural history of death.

I had picked up the knife and was closing it when the abrupt hiss of intaken breath behind me turned my own body momentarily rigid. I glanced over my shoulder and saw a middle-aged woman standing in the doorway with her legs apart. The look of horror on her plain face was so intense that it outlawed me to myself, as if she had really caught me in a shameful act. The knife sprang open in my hand as I turned and stood up. Then, the breath that she had taken and held came out in a high scream. I walked towards her and saw in detail the unplucked eyebrows raised on her lined forehead, the lines that ran down from the fleshy wings of her nose, deepened and curved by her smile of terror, the tense wrinkle across her hairy upper lip, the false upper teeth that slid down into the space between her parted lips and made even her fear ridiculous. The insane logic of the situation was so pressing that I felt almost compelled to kill her as she expected me to. Her screaming was intolerable. Nothing I could say would silence her. The knife was in my hand.

But I refused the role of murderer for which I had been cast. As I approached the doorway she cowered away from me and fell backwards on the floor. I closed the knife and went out the front door, leaving her sitting with her legs spraddled in front of her, her cotton print dress dragged up past her blue-veined thighs, her black mercerized stockings twisted around her thick ankles.

The maid on the next veranda was watching the house when I came out. I controlled the panic with which Mrs. Weather's servant had infected me and walked briskly but casually down the steps and sidewalk to the street, past the staring girl with the immobilized broom. A door across the street burst open suddenly, but I didn't turn my head to look. I turned the corner and made for the Packard. Before I reached it a woman shouted: "Stop him! Murder!" I jumped into the car and turned on the ignition. Then I realized that

Floraine Weather's car was no use to me if I wanted to get away.

As I got out, a big man in trousers and bathrobe came round the corner and ran heavily towards me. He had a white-lathered neck and a safety razor in his hand. I took Garland's gun out of my pocket and showed it to him. He stopped in his tracks and stood panting, his little razor clenched in his hand like a weapon. The maid with the broom appeared at the corner and called to him:

"Don't go near him, Mr. Terhune. He'll kill you."

"Throw down that gun," Mr. Terhune commanded me. His voice was husky and uneven.

Several other women joined the maid at the corner, howling and squealing when they saw me. "Come back, Terry," one of them cried. "Can't you see he's got a gun?"

For his age and weight, Mr. Terhune was a brave man. He walked towards me uncertainly but without halting, crouched forward slightly in his flapping bathrobe, like an old wrestler coming down the aisle to meet the unbeaten masked marvel.

I couldn't shoot him, I couldn't talk to him, I couldn't stop him. I turned and ran. Mr. Terhune ran after me, bellowing: "Stop! Murderer!"

By the time I reached the next corner he was half a block behind me, but there must have been a dozen people, men and women, strung out along the street in chase. More were streaming from the houses to join them. They made a confused, rapid chattering, like a pack of monkeys that has been frightened by a snake.

As soon as I was out of sight around the corner, I slowed to a quick walk and looked up and down the street. For the moment there was nobody to be seen. I went up the first driveway, beside a tall, red brick house built close to the street. Before I reached the closed garage at the end of the driveway, I heard shouts and footsteps at the corner. I ducked around the rear corner of the house and stood against the wall, wondering where to go from there. The running feet I had heard went by and on up the street, but more kept coming.

I detached myself from the wall and ran across the deep back yard, past a covered sandbox and a child's swing, through a row of leafless bushes that scratched at my clothes, over the high wooden fence. I crouched against the fence for a minute, looking ahead and listening behind me. The noise seemed to be fading away—at any rate coming no closer than the street. Ahead of me and to my right, a man came out the back of the house next door, buttoning his topcoat. He went into his garage and a minute later backed his car out. A little girl in a bib ran to the door and waved goodby to him. A woman with curlers in her hair came to the door behind the little girl and told her to get away from the open door, she'd catch cold. I watched these people with all the interest of a member of the family. They didn't see me.

When the door slammed finally shut, I stood up and walked across the muddy lawn towards the back porch of the house I had landed behind. There were sounds of movement in the back kitchen, and a woman's voice rose in a yell which froze me for a moment. What she said was: "Alec! Are you up yet? You don't want to be late for school."

There was a bicycle leaning against the back wall of the house beside the driveway. I climbed on, and coasted down the gentle slope to the street. After what seemed a long chase, I was back on Fenton Boulevard, half a block from Floraine Weather's front door. I tried to comfort myself with the reflection that a bicycle is a kind of disguise, which makes an old man look older and a young man look younger, but going back to that street was like diving into ice-cold water. Out of the tail of my eyes as I turned downtown, I saw women and children scattered like confetti on the sidewalks and porches of the next block. I gripped the rubber ends of the handle bars and pedaled hard away from them. A steady blast of cold air poured into my face and made my eyes water, and my feet sprinted round on the pedals. God knows where I was going, but I was going, and I felt almost good about it.

At the second corner I passed, my inflated mood was smashed like a paper bag. Mr. Terhune was slogging up the side street towards me, his bare, sweating belly bouncing over his trousers in front of him and his bathrobe flying out behind. I put down my head and kept going, but he saw me, brandished his safety razor like a talisman, and let out a breathless yell. The motley pack behind him took up the cry of murder. I looked back from the next corner and saw him waving his arms in the middle of the road. A car slowed down and he jumped on the running board. When I looked again he was crouched on the side of the accelerating car, pointing ahead like a manhunter in an old movie serial—a middle-aged householder tapped by destiny and rising to the occasion with everything he had. I began to dislike him intensely, and even to regret I hadn't shot him in the foot. But all I could do now was pedal for my life, which I did.

Ahead of me and somewhere out of sight a desultory whining formed itself into a steady tone that mounted gradually to a high shriek, so loud that it dominated the morning. As if to disclaim its threat, the siren died away and lost itself. But then it recovered its voice, nearer and louder. When I was passing the Presbyterian Church a police car turned into the street two blocks ahead of me and came towards me howling. I turned up the driveway at the side of the church, applied the brakes and found that there weren't any, skidded on the gravelly sidewalk, and coasted shakily around the back of the church. The back door was locked. Somebody fired a shot on the other side of the building. I picked up the bicycle and threw it through the stained-glass window as a diversion, then ran around the corner of the church.

The next building was the Public Library, and memory or instinct led me around the back of it to the other side. There was a rusty old fire escape here, with an iron ladder nine or ten feet from the ground. I jumped for the bottom rung, went up hand over hand till I got a foothold, and climbed to the platform at the second story. The window was partly open, and the room inside looked deserted. From the direction of the church I heard a rhythmic pounding and then a smash, as if they had forced the back door. I hoisted my legs over the sill and locked the window behind me. I stood against the wall for a minute or two, breathing the peaceful smell of furniture oil and old books, and listening to my heart slow down.

Three of the four walls of the big square room were lined with bookshelves. Against the fourth there was a semicircular counter with a swinging door at the side. A sign propped on the counter said: "Children's Department: Circulating Desk: Hours from 3 to 5:30 P.M." I breathed easier. It looked as if nobody would be here in the morning. There was a bulletin board beside the open door, and I scanned the notices nervously. The largest was a hand-painted invitation to: "Come and Hear Miss Flicka Runymede's weekly Series of Readings from Andersen and Grimm"; Thursday's tales were to be "The Little Match Girl" and "The Ugly Duckling."

A pair of dragging feet began to ascend the creaky stairs on the other side of the door. I ran across the room on my toes, vaulted the circulation desk, and sat down behind it between piles of books. The footsteps dragged across the landing and the door squeaked open. "That's goshdarned funny," an old man's voice said to itself: "I was goshdarned sure I opened that window this morning." I began to regret the impulse that had made me close it.

The feet crossed the floor so slowly, as if time itself had creeping paralysis, that I wanted to get behind him and push.

"I'll be goldarn goshdarned," the old man sputtered to himself. "I didn't even unlock the goldamned thing." I heard him fling the window wide open. "This time, stay open, see? I got more to do than going around opening windows the whole Jehosophat day."

Somebody shouted outside: "Hey, there! Did you see anybody running past here?"

"Nope," the old man said. "I ain't seen nobody no-how. Who you looking for?"

"An escaped murderer. An insane killer that killed a woman up the street."

"A murderer?" the old man quavered at the window.

"You think I'm kidding, grandpa? Did you see him or hear anything?"

"I didn't hear nobody or nothing."

"Well, if you do, just sing out. We'll be around here searching."

"Certainly will, officer. Yes, sir. But I hope to Moses he don't come around here."

The old man's feet recrossed the room in a syncopated shuffle and creaked back down the steps. When I could no longer hear him on the stairs, I climbed out from behind the counter and followed him out the door. Because I didn't dare go back to the windows, I had to find another way out. By leaning on the banister and shifting my weight gradually from step to step, I kept the stairs from creaking. There was a landing half-way down, from which I could see that the stairs led into the main entrance hall of the library. I was weighing the chances of making a run for it when I saw the back of a blue policeman's uniform at the front door.

Opening off the landing was a door with a ground-glass window which bore the lettering: "Storage Department." I tried the knob, found that it gave, and went through into a dark corridor. At the end of the corridor was a second door that opened into a long, low room. Shelves of yellowing newspapers and books with worn bindings rose from floor to ceiling between narrow aisles. I had a wild impulse to browse among the old newspapers, perhaps to find an account of my father's murder, or his wedding, or the last party he threw. It was the impulse of a man who had no time to lose and nothing to gain by saving it.

At the far end of the room, between green-blinded windows, there was a shelf labeled: "These Books Are Not To Be Circulated." Some of the titles I noticed were *Gargantua and Pantagruel*, *The Sentimental Education*, *To Have and Have Not*, *The Wild Palms*. It was somehow comforting to know that the good people of the town that supported Kerch were protected against the lubricity of Rabelais, the immorality of Flaubert, the viciousness of Hemingway, and the degradation of Faulkner.

There was a circular iron staircase in the corner to my right, leading down into darkness. I descended by it to the next floor, where I found myself among dim bookshelves, probably the main stacks of the library. The iron stairs led down further, and I followed them for two more flights and felt a cement floor under my feet. The basement windows were small and placed high in the concrete wall, but I started towards them to see if they opened. The longer I stayed where I was, the more thoroughly I'd be encircled and the more certainly caught in the end.

Before I reached the first of the row of windows, the polished black leather legs of a motorcycle cop strode across it. The sight of them was like a blow in the face, which sent me backwards across the room to the opposite wall. I backed into a door, found the latch, and went through it into the next room. This was a toilet and washroom, lit by a naked bulb which hung on a cord from the ceiling above a cracked mirror and sink.

So many faces had passed, so many things had happened before my eyes in the last twelve hours that I had forgotten I had a face myself. When I looked at it in the clouded mirror, I would have been willing to settle for none. I was pale under the streaks of dirt, and the black beard coming out on my cheeks and chin made me look paler. There was a dark abrasion on the left angle of my jaw. Worst of all were my eyes, a blue sludge color framed in pink, as if I had spent the night carousing and having a hell of a time. I didn't like my face. It didn't have any frank, boyish charm at all. With the dark-red spatter on my shirt, I looked like a refugee from a murder rap. A little crazy, too, in a sly way.

I washed my face in cold water and combed the front part of my hair with a pocket comb. The back of my head was a stiff and tangled mass which hurt to the touch. Then I cautiously opened the door and looked through into the next room.

It was a windowless cell with several open lockers along one wall, and along the other a row of hooks from which hung two or three hats and topcoats. I tried each of the coats and found a worn Oxford gray that would go over my shoulders without tearing. The greasy old fedora that went with it was too big for me, but I needed a hat. My own had been lost somewhere, I didn't know when. So I jammed it on my head with the brim resting on my ears. To complete the disguise, I found a dusty pair of rimless spectacles on the top shelf of one of the open lockers, and a big leather book in another. The spectacles blurred my vision, even after I had wiped them, but that was all to the good. Maybe they'd make my eyes look different.

I went back through the washroom and peered over the spectacles into the mirror. I recognized myself all right, but perhaps I looked a little like an impecunious scholar, and even a trifle Jewish. I hoped that native fascism hadn't progressed in the city to the point where the police would think I was a suspicious character because I looked Jewish.

I retraced my steps across the basement, up the spiral staircase, through the storage department, and out onto the landing above the entrance hall. The policeman was still standing with his back to the door. I felt shaky and conspicuous, like an inexperienced diver about to go off the high board for the first time. But I hunched my shoulders in what I hoped would look like a scholar's stoop, and went down the stairs to the door.

I pulled open the heavy glass door and mumbled: "Excuse me, officer," to the policeman's broad back.

"Pardon me." He stepped aside out of my way.

I walked down the stone steps in front of him, using all my self-control to keep from breaking into a run. There was a police car parked at the curb, which contained a man in plain clothes listening to his short-wave radio. There were two more policemen and a group of civilians on the corner in front of the church. I crossed the street in front of the parked car and walked away in the opposite direction from the church. When I reached the corner I refrained from looking back. I turned downtown and started walking faster. Main Street would be a tough gantlet to run, but the only person I could go to for help lived in the Harvey Apartments, on the other side of the business district. And even she was an off-chance.

I passed a number of people and none of them paid any attention to me. The life of the city was going on as if Floraine Weather had never died, or never lived. There was a bus parked on the next corner, headed in the direction I wanted to go, and I joined the line of passengers and got on.

"How much?" I said to the driver.

"Five cents in the downtown zone. Say, it sure looks as if you're gonna read a book."

"Yeah."

I found an unoccupied seat in the back and opened the book in my lap. It was St. Augustine's *City of God*, in Latin. At the next stop, which was Main Street, most of the passengers got off and left me feeling kind of naked. I stayed where I was, pretending to be engrossed in Latin I couldn't read.

"Hey, bud," the driver said. "You with the book. It costs you another fare if you want to stay on."

"Where do you go from here?"

"To Farmers' Square and up Fenton Boulevard. That where you want to go?"

I got off in a hurry, hugging my book. The policeman on the corner glanced at me curiously, looked away for a moment at the traffic, and looked back at me with renewed interest. I went in at the first open door I came to. It happened to be a barbershop.

The barber standing beside an empty chair at the back snapped a towel like a lion tamer who has seen a lion. "Shave or haircut, sir?"

My nerves recoiled at the thought of spending half an hour in a barber's chair, with a policeman just outside. "I just came in to get some hair tonic. I've been troubled by dandruff."

"Would you just mind taking your hat off, let me look at your scalp?"

"Yes, I would. I just want you to sell me a bottle of hair tonic."

"Very well, sir. O.K. What kind would you wish?"

"That kind." I pointed at a bottle with a purple label.

"Yes, sir. Virility Violet. Very effective for dandruff, Virility Violet. That will be one dollar, and three cents tax."

I set my book down on a table and took out my wallet to pay him. As I did so, I glanced over my shoulder and saw the policeman watching me through the window.

"Is there a back way out of here?"

"Yes, sir. Right through there. You sick or something?"

"Yes," I said, and left him.

"Hey, you forgot your tonic! You forgot your book—"

The door closing behind me cut off his voice, but I could still hear the police whistle in the street.

Chapter 17

The rat in the maze was getting tired but as the experiment proceeded, the stimuli were becoming more powerful. I ran down a dark corridor, saw daylight under an ill-fitting door, and came out in an alley. Forty or fifty feet from the back door of the barbershop an old delivery truck stood shuddering, with its back doors swinging open. There was nobody in sight just then, but there soon would be. I sprinted for the truck and crawled in. Behind the driver's seat there was a pile of old burlap bags, and I covered myself with them and lay still, breathing the odor of rancid coffee beans.

In a few seconds I heard somebody come out and, with a straining grunt, lift something heavy onto the back of the truck. Then a door slammed open and several pairs of running feet came down the alley.

"Did you see a man in a dark-gray coat? He just came out of the back of the barbershop."

"Not me, officer," a boy's voice said. "I been loading this here truck and I didn't see nobody."

"He must've gone the other way," the barber said. "Out to Randall Street. I thought there was something funny about that character—"

"Who?" asked the delivery boy.

"He's a murderer. He chopped up a woman into little pieces."

"Jesus Christ!"

"Let's go!" the policeman said. "Maybe we can head him off."

Their heavy footsteps went away like a receding doom. The boy ran into the building and left me the action of my heart to listen to. After a while he came out and climbed into the driver's seat. The idling motor took hold and the truck began to move.

"Hey, wait a minute!" somebody yelled, and the driver slammed brakes on the truck and my breathing. My hand moved up my thigh, across my hip, and found the gun in my pocket.

"What you want, Pete?"

"You goin' up past Gormlay's?"

"Yeah. I can drop you there. Hop in."

The door was flung open and the other seat creaked under weight. Two people in the front made it too bad for somebody. Probably me. But at least the truck was moving again, away from the danger zone.

"That was a pretty slinky little blonde I seen you with last night," the driver said.

"Her?" The other boy's voice was scornful. "I can take her or leave her alone. But she's crazy about me, and that always helps. I give her a break every now and then."

"Any time you don't need her, you can drop her on my doorstep. I got a use for slinky little blondes."

"I thought you was makin' out with Rose?"

"Sure, I see her regular. But what I always say, variety, you know, the spice of life. I figure I'm a little young to settle down for keeps. I wanta look 'em over first. Like in business now."

The truck bumped down a curb and turned left into a roaring stream of traffic. Minute by minute it was getting harder for me to lie still. Though I was probably getting enough air through the loosely woven burlap, I had the feeling that I wasn't. I felt like a Turk in a sack on his last ride to the Bosphorus.

"What's it got to do with business? Pleasure is what I call it."

"Look at it this way," the driver said. "I got something to sell, in a way. Does a guy that's got something to sell let it go to the first bidder? No sir, not the way I do business! It's the same with a dame. My plan is to look 'em over first and take the best I can get."

"You better watch out you don't knock Rose up, then."

"Don't worry about me. She knows her way around. And if she didn't, I could always scrape up fifty bucks. Do it the scientific way, is what I always say."

"Yeah, science is a great thing. It musta been tough on a girl before they had all this modern science."

"I wonder what would make a guy cut a woman up like that," the driver said.

"That guy the cops were after? Jeez, I dunno. Mr. Hirschman said he heard over the radio it was for revenge. She was his stepmother or sumpin', and treated him terrible when he was a kid."

"I betchit was sex. Take most of these murders, sex is at the bottom of it. Sex is what makes a man nuts. That's the chief reason I go out with girls all the time."

"Because you're nuts?"

"Hell, no! Because I don't wanna go nuts. I read a book, you gotta have a satisfactory sex life. That's what it said in the book."

"You can let me off at the red light. I don't get it about sex making a guy nuts. It never made me feel any different one way or the other."

"Yeah, but over a period of time," the boy at the wheel said. "Over a period of time. So long, see you in church."

"Not me you won't!" The door opened and slammed, and the driver started to sing *Don't Be a Baby, Baby* to himself and me.

The truck went into gear and turned left again. After a couple of minutes the sounds of traffic became intermittent. The truck turned and bumped up a curb, moved over an uneven pavement, and came to a stop in a quiet place. The driver got out, leaving the engine rattling, and opened the doors at the back. The rear springs squeaked and he grunted again as he lifted something heavy off the truck. His footsteps staggered away and a door slammed.

I threw off the sacks and slid off the back of the truck into another alley. The spectacles were still on my nose, blurring my vision. I tore them off and threw them into an empty carton at the end of a loading platform. Then I went out of the alley the way we had come in, and turned south along the street. It was a street of dirty little bars, four-dollar-permanent parlors, marked-down millinery shops, unappetizing delicatessens—the frayed hem of the business district. In the next block, among the two-bit hotels and store-front tabernacles, I felt even more at home with my sprouting beard and ruined clothes. Nearly everybody I met bore the stamp of poverty on faces strained thin or coarsened by the exigencies of marginal life, and nobody gave me a second glance.

Some kind of dead reckoning guided me east at the next corner and south again at the one after that. I went down a lane along a high board fence at the rear of a row of tenements, and came out behind the Harvey Apartments. She won't be home, I told myself, to take the curse off disappointment. If she is, she won't want you cluttering up her day. In any case, you've got no right to run to her with your troubles. She's got enough of her own.

But the pride had been scared and beaten out of me. The open air and the bright sunlight frightened me the way a child is frightened of the dark. I felt as naked and desperate as a worm in the middle of a concrete road, nosing blindly for a place to hole up.

A plain-white card bearing the signature Carla Kaufman was in the number-three mailbox, and I found the corresponding apartment on the ground floor at the rear. I knocked softly on the door and waited. A middle-aged woman in a cotton wrapper opened the door across the hall and picked up a quart of milk.

"Carla's never up this early in the morning," she said. "She works late."

"I know." I kept my face to the door so that she couldn't get a good view of me. "Thank you." She closed her door.

I knocked again, and after an interval, slippered feet whispered inside the apartment and the door opened a crack. Her dark hair was tangled and her blue eyes puffed with sleep. She had on a blue quilted robe over blue pajamas. She looked at me uncertainly for a moment, as if she didn't recognize me.

"Remember me?" I said. "The bad penny?"

She yawned, a wide, childish yawn and rubbed her fists into her eyes.

"May I come in?"

"I guess so." She stepped back and I closed the door behind me. "What is this, anyway?"

I realized suddenly that she and I were almost complete strangers, that I was bringing nothing but bad trouble to a girl I hardly knew, and the realization tied my tongue. "I shouldn't have come here," I muttered. Circumstances the night before had made it easy for me to talk to her, but now she had retreated into a private identity.

"It's kind of early in the morning for visiting, isn't it? Christ, I never get to bed before four."

"I didn't come to visit you. The police are after me."

"I heard somebody got thrown out of the club last night. Was that you?"

"It was me, all right, but that isn't what's worrying me. Kerch framed me for a murder. He killed Mrs. Weather and hung it on me."

"No!" She looked at me incredulously, and her morning pallor grew paler still.

"Don't tell me things like that don't happen. They do when Kerch is around."

"Did you get to see Allister, like I told you?"

"Yeah, but he fell down on me. He's got a better front and a high-class line of talk, but he's as bad as the rest."

"No, he's not," she said flatly. "He's a good man."

"He may be kind to his mother, I wouldn't know. I came to you because you were the only one I could think of."

She was frightened, but she did her best to hide it from me. "I'm glad you came to me. I didn't think I'd ever see you again, you know that? But I don't know what to do." She emitted a little snort that was halfway between a laugh and a sob.

"Just let me stay here for a while. I wouldn't last long on the streets. There's nobody else lives with you?"

"No. I told you I lived by myself. Take off your coat and hat, Johnny. Make yourself at home."

"You're a good girl. I suppose you know you're taking a big risk?"

"Yeah, and so early in the morning, too," she said in her ironic monotone. "I ought to murder you myself for waking me up so early in the morning."

"Don't use that word, 'murder.' Use any other word instead."

"What's the matter, you got the jitters, Johnny?" Her vivacity was a little forced but it was better than none.

"I won't try to tell you about it," I said as I struggled out of the tight coat I had stolen. "If I didn't have the jitters, there'd be something the matter with my head."

She hung my coat and hat in a closet which opened off the tiny hall, and led me into the living-room.

"Better pull down the blinds," I said, but she was already on her way to the windows.

She switched on a floor lamp by an armchair. "Sit down. You look as if you've been up all night."

"I have."

"Go to sleep if you want to. I have only the one bed, but you can have it."

"I couldn't sleep. But thanks for being so damn nice."

"For God's sake, don't get sentimental! You had any breakfast yet?"

"No, I'm not hungry."

"Don't kid yourself. Just give me three minutes to slip into some clothes, and I'll make you breakfast."

She went into the bedroom and closed the door behind her. I sat and thought of nothing, but a little spring of good feeling had begun to bubble up inside me. She was a good girl with a nice solid core. I felt like an alley cat that has been taken in out of the cold and given warm milk, except that an alley cat is never tempted to shed tears of gratitude. She was right. I was getting sentimental. And as sometimes happens for no good reason when you're beaten down and exhausted, a node of heat had formed in my loins and was branching through my body. I caught myself waiting second by second for the bedroom door to open again. "What's the matter, Weather," I asked myself, "you got no shame?"

She came out looking brisk, with her hair pinned up and an apron over her dress. Her only concession to my sex was a trace of lipstick on her mouth. But the stiff cotton front of the high-collared dress curved breathtakingly over her bosom and fell away into a tight-belted waist I could have put my hands around.

"I like you in that dress," I said lamely.

"No kidding?" She looked at me and smiled. "You're not talking as if you had the jitters now."

"You cured 'em." I stood up and moved toward her.

She moved away with a dancer's bodily tact. "What you need is food, my boy. You better stay out of the kitchen. Somebody might see you from the back porch."

She let the door swing to and left me alone again. I heard the rattle of a pan on the stove, grease sizzling, eggs being broken.

"You want 'em sunny side up?" she called.

"Easy over," I called back.

While water ran into a coffee percolator and the eggs sputtered in hot grease, I looked around the room. There wasn't much to look at: a chesterfield and matching armchair, a coffee-table, a portable record player on a stand with a pile of records beside it, a magazine rack containing a *Mademoiselle*, a couple of copies of *Life*, and a cheap reprint of a historical romance; but as it was, the room was crowded. There were no pictures on the wall, and no photograph anywhere. Either she hadn't lived there long, or she hadn't intended to stay. Even a migratory bird left more permanent traces than she had in her living-room.

She came through the swinging door with a wooden tray in one hand, a pot of coffee in the other. She set down the tray on the coffee-table beside me, and I saw that it contained a plate of four fried eggs and a pile of toast.

"This looks wonderful," I said. "Aren't you going to eat, too?"

"Not this early. I'll have some coffee, though. You want your coffee black?"

"Very black."

I stabbed an egg and discovered that I was hungry after all.

She half-sat on the arm of the other chair with one slender knee swinging loose, and watched me over the rim of her coffee cup.

"You want some more?" she said after a while. "I only made four on account of you not being hungry."

"I was wrong." I finished the toast with my coffee. "But I'm not hungry any more. I almost feel good, in fact."

"I feel pretty good, too. God knows why."

"Don't you ever get lonely?" I don't know why I said it. Perhaps it was the homelessness of the room, or her attitude on the chair arm, perched like a bird waiting for a signal to take flight.

"I don't think so," she said after a pause. "I never thought about it much. Maybe I'm a kind of hermit. I get awfully tired of all the people at the club, having to talk to them, and everything."

"Anybody would, but I didn't exactly mean that. I mean when you come home, and probably make your own supper, and eat by yourself."

"I often eat with Sonia down the hall. And sometimes with Francie Sontag. She's right upstairs. I go out a lot to eat, too. It's no fun cooking for yourself. You know, I got a hell of a bang out of making breakfast for you. I'd hate to think I was the homemaker type." She let herself fall back into the chair in a movement that was deliberately hoydenish, but with such unconscious grace that it looked right.

"Maybe you are, though."

She kicked her legs restlessly over the arm, then succumbed to the seriousness of her thoughts: "It's not much fun doing anything for yourself. I spend about an hour a day fixing my nails, and another hour on my hair, but I just do it to put in time. There's no real kick in it. I used to hate the dirty work around Grandfather's flat, but there was some kind of kick in it that I don't get when I clean up this dump. Sometimes I sit on my tail for three or four hours without lifting a finger. Maybe I'm just plain lazy."

"Maybe you are. Or maybe you're lonely."

"You're a serious-minded son of a bitch, aren't you?"

"Not particularly. That's just the way you affect me. I don't think you live the way you should."

"Now, Johnny." She spoke lightly but with an undertone of resentment. "You're not going to start harping on that again?"

"I mean you shouldn't live by yourself like this. You said you like doing things for other people. Why don't you give yourself a chance to?"

"That's true. I'd rather do up another girl's hair than do my own." She gave me a quizzical look that was a half smile. "You don't mean I should start living with somebody? I get plenty of that kind of offers."

"Maybe I don't know what I mean."

"Half the women in these flats have got men supporting them. But it's no damn good, not for the women anyway. Practically every one of them turns into a lush. All except Francie and a couple of others. They go soft, and get fussy and worried, like a hen without any chicks. Then they start drinking in the afternoon, and pretty soon they're drinking in the forenoon. Like Mrs. Williams across the hall. You know what she has for breakfast every morning? Three slugs of rye. Every two or three months her man doesn't show up for a week or so, and she drinks so hard she gets the d.t.'s. They make me mad, the way they throw themselves away, but I can't tell them anything."

"You're not even throwing yourself away," I said. "You're sitting and waiting and letting your best years go by. Waiting for nothing."

She drew in her legs and sat up with them under her. "I know it, but you don't have to say it. Half the time I'm so blue I can't even listen to music on the record player. It doesn't do any good to tell me things like that. It only makes things worse."

"Why the hell don't you snap out of it?"

Her mouth twisted into an ugly shape. "Why the hell don't you mind your own business?"

My own temper flared up to meet hers, but subsided almost immediately. Already a shadow of regret had softened her face, and her teeth plucked at her lower lip.

"I didn't tell you that Joe Sault's dead, did I?"

"You know you didn't. Why are you telling me now?" Her eyes and voice were as calm as could be, but I got the impression that perhaps she was watching herself, guarding against an emotion she didn't want to admit.

"I'm not sure. It could be the thing you needed to start you off on a fresh track. You know, a new page in the book."

"It doesn't make any difference to me at all." The flatness of her tone illustrated her meaning. "I haven't had anything to do with him for nearly two years. I told you last night how I felt about him."

"Still, I think you're better off with him dead."

"Did you kill him?" In her voice there was the suppressed excitement of a woman who thinks she has guessed the answer to a question, and finds it somehow flattering to herself.

"No," I said emphatically. "Kerch beat him to death."

"Oh." Conflicting emotions made a delicate shadow play in her eyes.

"I never thought I'd feel sorry for Joey, but I did."

"I don't," she said, too readily. "Does Francie know?"

"I don't think so."

"It's going to jolt her. She was always fond of him. God knows why. He was her youngest brother, and she practically brought him up." She was silent for a while, her eyes unfocused in thought. "That wasn't true, what I said about not being sorry for him. I am sorry. It's

funny. I thought I hated him so much." She added irrel-
evantly: "You don't like me a little bit, do you?"

"I like you. I think we could understand each other.
I've felt kind of lonely and unsettled, the same way you
do, ever since my family broke up. I could never get
close to my mother. She was all right and she did what
she could, but I couldn't talk to her. It really didn't
bother me much when she died."

"It broke me up when my mother died," she said. "I
guess I never got over it. But she was different. I could
talk to her about anything. The things that Grandfather
said never seemed to make any real sense to me. He's
supposed to be pretty clever, but he gets all tangled up
in words. He's got his head in the clouds, he reminds
me of Allister. Since my mother died I haven't really
had anybody I could talk to—or that I wanted to talk
to."

"Do you know Allister pretty well?"

"I told you I knew him." She seemed unwilling to
tell me any more. "How old were you when your
mother died?"

"I was seventeen, but I'd been running around pretty
much on my own for a long time before that. She left
me enough money to go to college for a couple of
years, but that didn't mean much to me. I went to three
different colleges, and I never felt I belonged to anything, then or after. My last couple of years in the
army were pretty good, though. I got to be a sergeant,
and our platoon made a sharp team. But most of them
got knocked off at Malmédy, in the Battle of the
Bulge. I guess you've heard about that."

"Naturally. You must think I'm a complete stupe."

"I don't think you're half as stupid as you try to pre-
tend to be. But you need somebody to snap you out of
it."

"Aren't you wonderful?" she said with a smile.
"You're sitting here with the cops looking for you, tired
out and beaten up, and all you think about is how I
should run my life. Aren't you worried about
yourself?"

"Not particularly. I'm too far gone to worry about."

"Oh no. You're not." Her bare legs uncoiled from under her and brought her across to me in two running steps. "We've got to do something. Just tell me what to do, and I'll do it."

She kissed my cheek in a warm, flurried way. My arms went around her legs as she stood in front of me, and my fingers pressed the cool skin behind her knees.

"Don't," she said, and pushed her hands downward against my shoulders.

I didn't believe she meant it. My embrace moved up her thighs.

"Don't," she said. "Please."

The strain in her voice made me look up at her face. The angry embarrassment I saw there seemed more than half genuine. I let go of her, and she stepped back precipitately into the middle of the room.

"You mustn't," she said with relief. "I couldn't let you make love to me in the morning. We've got to think of what to do."

"I haven't any ideas. Have you?"

"You're the one who should snap out of it. Wait a minute—"

"What's the matter?"

"Hush! There's somebody coming up the back steps."

Chapter 18

I listened, and heard the quick footsteps on the boards of the back porch. The girl went to the kitchen door, opened it slightly, and peered through.

"It's all right," she said. "It's Allister."

"Allister!" I got up and moved towards the hall. "I better get out of here."

"Wait, he's not after you. He's always coming here."

"To see you?"

"Don't be silly. I suppose I might as well tell you, he comes to see Francie Sontag. He supports Francie."

The footsteps had ascended another flight of steps, and could no longer be heard.

"Why didn't you tell me? You talked as if Allister was a saintly character."

"I did not. Anyway, I don't hold it against a man if he keeps a woman. He can't marry her, because his wife won't give him a divorce. And he doesn't run around with other women. I feel sorry for him, the way he has to sneak up the back way to see her."

"It doesn't seem to be much of a secret."

"Not around here, but we don't try to make anything of it. It's just that if it got around among the respectable people—" she gave the phrase an ironic twist—"it would finish him in politics."

"Wait a minute." I was remembering the man's voice in Francie Sontag's apartment, the man's gray coat on the arm of her chesterfield. "Was Allister with her last night?"

"How should I know?"

"I heard a man in her apartment—"

"It could have been Joe Sault. He sleeps there sometimes. Slept, I mean."

"No, it wasn't his voice."

"It was probably Allister's then. She doesn't mess around with anybody else—she hasn't for a couple of years."

My mind put two and two together and got a five-figure number. "What's Francie Sontag's phone number?"

"23748. Why? I can go and get him if you want to talk to him."

"Do you think I can trust him not to call the police?"

"If you can convince him you were framed. I've seen him help more than one fellow out of a bad spot."

"Go and get him, then," I said. "I'll take another chance."

"Another chance?"

"It'd take too long to explain. Ask him to come down, but don't tell Francie I'm here."

"Don't worry."

As she was leaving I said: "You don't have a razor, do you?"

"Not the kind you use. It's a little round one. I'll show you."

"Mind if I try shaving with it? My story'll sound better if I've got a clean face."

"Come in here." She led me through the disordered bedroom into a small bathroom that opened off it. She rummaged in the cupboard above the sink, handed me a toy-like safety razor, and laughed at the look on my face.

"You haven't any shaving soap?"

"I just use ordinary soap. I'm sorry."

While she went upstairs I took off my coat and shirt, washed, and shaved painfully. I felt better then. The engines of my body started to reverse themselves again, shifting from the defensive to the offensive. I began to outline the tongue-lashing I intended to give Allister, and to wonder again where Kerch was.

The hall door opened when I was putting on my coat, and the two of them came into the apartment.

"I don't like this, Carla," Allister was saying. "Who

is it that wants to see me? You know I don't like anybody to see me here."

"It can't be helped this time," she said.

I crossed the bedroom and stepped into the livingroom.

He stood up when he saw me. "My God, man, how did you get here?"

"Car, bicycle, truck, and foot."

"What on earth has been happening? Francie was just telling me about your phone call. It was you, wasn't it?"

"You're damn right it was, but it's a little late for you to be hearing about it. Sault is dead and buried."

"Sault!" Allister said incredulously. "Did you say Joe Sault?"

"Sault's dead, and Floraine Weather's dead. And every cop in town is looking for me."

"I know that. I just came from the police station."

"If you had come when I phoned you, you could have fixed Kerch for good. But maybe you don't want to fix him?"

"Don't jump to conclusions, Weather. I didn't get your message until five minutes ago."

"Maybe it was convenient for you not to get the message."

Allister went pale and his whole body trembled with rage, but he kept his voice steady. "Can you listen to reason, Weather? I was out for hours, walking the streets. She told me about it as soon as she got in touch with me. Surely I haven't given you any reason to believe that I've been working with Kerch."

"You've got a chance to prove it now. Whistle your cops off my trail—"

"I'm afraid I haven't the power. I'll do what I can."

"All right, here's something you can do. Kerch committed murder at the Wildwood Inn last night. Twice. Garland and Rusty Jahnke helped him. If I hit them as hard as I think I did, they're still out at the Wildwood. You know where that is?"

"Yes."

"Garland and Rusty are on the floor in the back kitchen. Are there any cops you can trust at all?"

"There's Hanson. He's a good man. And maybe two or three others."

"Take them, then, and round up Kerch's accomplices. There's plenty of evidence against them in that kitchen, and Sault's buried in the back yard. That's something you can do if Kerch hasn't got you hogtied."

"I'll do it. Are you going to stay here?"

"I haven't decided. But for God's sake, don't tell the police I'm here! For Carla's sake, at least."

"He wouldn't do that," Carla said. "You've got him all wrong."

"I promise you I'll be discreet. Good luck."

"Good luck to you."

"You see?" Carla said when the door had closed behind him. "I told you you could trust Allister."

"He hasn't done anything yet. I'm waiting for him to produce. You notice he didn't say anything about rounding up Kerch."

"I think he's afraid of him."

"Why should everybody be afraid of Kerch? I'm not."

"I know you're not." She put both her hands on my upper arm and squeezed hard. "I think you're wonderful; I really mean it this time. You never stop fighting, do you?"

"Like hell I'm wonderful!" But she made me feel that way. "Kerch is a nasty sort of organism, but he's the kind of thing that decent people brush off and forget about. How he ever got this town by the tail, I can't figure out."

"He's evil," she said with intensity. "There's nothing he wouldn't do. That's why decent people like Allister can't cope with him. He plays a game without any rules at all."

"I've forgotten most of the rules myself. I wouldn't mind playing another rubber with Kerch." A desperate plan was forming in my mind. If I could get Kerch by himself, now that Garland and Rusty were out of the picture, if I could get him by himself in the back room of the Cathay Club. . . .

"From what you said last night," I said, "I got the idea that Kerch liked you. Is that right?"

"I don't think he likes anybody. He wants to make love to me, if that's what you mean—his idea of making love."

"Would he come if you called him, do you think?"

"Here?" An undercurrent of panic changed her face.

"No, not here—the Cathay Club. Would he come out there if you asked him to?"

"I don't know. I don't want to try, either. I can't bear him."

"You wouldn't have to bear him. I'll get there before he does and meet him there, instead of you. He doesn't know there's any connection between you and me. I'll show him stranger love-making than he ever dreamed of."

"You said you couldn't go on the streets. How would you get out there?"

"Have you got a car I can borrow? I should be able to make it in a car."

"Yeah, I've got an old coupé." Then her voice recovered its strength, as if she had made a decision that released energy inside her. "I'll drive you. You can ride in the trunk compartment."

"You'd be taking a chance—"

"I'm not afraid to take a chance. I'll bring the car around, and you can slip out the back door."

"There's no chance that he'd be out at the club now?"

"He never goes out there in the morning. I'll make sure, though."

She went to the phone in the hall and rang the Cathay Club. Nobody answered, which suited me. Then, she called the Palace Hotel and asked for Kerch's suite. I stood behind her and saw that the hand which held the receiver was trembling.

"Go away," she said impatiently. "I can't talk to him with you right here."

I stepped into the living-room and closed the door. I

couldn't hear what she said, but I could follow the in-
tonations of her voice. It moved from a teasing coyness
through soft persuasion and unexpected delight, ending
on a note of gentle anticipation. She had done what I
wanted her to do, and done it beautifully, but my feel-
ings were mixed. Women had so many emotional
strata, you were always breaking through a layer you
thought you knew and finding yourself in an atmosphere that was hard to breathe, a situation that was
quite new and a little frightening.

When she came back into the room, I saw how
much the conversation had taken out of her. She was
pale again, and breathing quickly. Her mouth had lost
its firm line. I walked towards her and put my arms
around her. Her body rested hard against me from
breast to knee, but her mouth made no response to my
kiss. Her eyes were open and perfectly calm and cool.
Suddenly she closed them and gave me the sweet and
terrible gift of her tongue. A slip-stream wind blew
away time and space. We were lost and holding to each
other in a new element as powerful and wild as a
breaking wave carrying us in to shore. We swayed and
almost fell.

"We mustn't," she said. "It makes me so weak I
can't even stand."

"You make me feel strong. You're like the other half
of my body."

"That's a crazy thing to say."

"It's not so crazy. You know the story that ever
pair of lovers was originally one person."

"Uh-uh. Aren't I ignorant?"

"Anyway, that's the story. The people in the world
are really just halves of people. Everybody is looking
for his other half. When he finds it, it's love. The whole
person. We're like that."

"Are we?" It was a rhetorical question which meant
that she didn't believe in any kind of love. "It's a pretty
story."

"We fit, don't we? Like the two halves of an apple."

"And an apple a day keeps the doctor away?"

"Don't be so damn cynical. It makes me want to wring your neck."

"But that would be suicide, the way you tell it." She kissed my cheek and broke my embrace. "Let's go, John. You said you wanted to get there before he does."

She brought her car around to the back steps, and I had an uncomfortable ride in the rear compartment— uncomfortable, but safe. When she raised the door, the car was parked in the deserted parking lot behind the Cathay Club. She unlocked the back entrance, let me in, and closed the door behind me. The windowless hall outside Kerch's office was pitch dark.

"You'd better go away and leave me here," I said. "You don't want to be here when Kerch comes."

"When he sees my car, he'll come in. I can go up to his room."

"You'd be safer if you went home."

"I'll be all right upstairs. You take care of yourself."

"Worry about Kerch," I said. "So long. You've got a lot of guts."

"Don't kid yourself, I'm scared. But maybe there's something in that fairy story you told me. It makes me feel good to be around you."

"Beat it. There's a car coming."

I saw her shadow for a moment against gray light at the end of the hall. Then the door closed and shut me into darkness again. I took Garland's automatic out of my pocket and made it ready to fire. The darkness was so thick I could hardly breathe it. But two or three facts were as clear in my head as objects under a searchlight. This was my last chance. If Kerch was alone I could break him down. If there was another man with him, I would have to kill the other man.

A heavy car crackled across the gravel, paused briefly, and backed to a stop just outside the door. A car door was shut. Slow footsteps came up to the door, and the door opened. I hesitated a second too long, making sure that there was nobody with him, nobody sitting in the car. He saw me and backed outside, slamming the door in my face. He let out a violent cry of "Help!"

Then I was on him, my hand twisting his collar into the soft flesh of his neck. His pearl-gray hat fell off and rolled in the dirt. He stuck out his thick tongue at me, and his protuberant eyes seemed almost ready to leap from his head like live slugs. A thin current of breath whistled shrilly in his throat.

I half carried and half dragged him through the door into the hall. There I loosened my hold on his neck and pressed the gun into the roll of fat which girdled his hips. I frisked him, finding no gun.

"Unlock your office. We have things to talk over."

"I have no key," he said hoarsely.

"Then I'll break it down, using your head for a battering-ram." I depressed his head and brought it in sharp contact with the door.

"I'll unlock it." He found the key and did.

"Turn on the light," I said. He turned on the light and I closed the door.

"You're a frightful fool, Weather," he began. "You have no chance whatever of getting away with this—"

I hit his jaw, hard enough to knock him down but not out. "Don't be urbane. Now, stand up."

He sat on the floor with his legs spread, looking up at me blankly.

"I said stand up! You don't know how to take orders." I put my hand inside his collar and jerked him to his feet.

"This is ridiculous—"

I hit him between the eyes, a little harder this time. He staggered back halfway across the room and fell on the couch. He lay where he was, with open eyes. Something in the posture of his gross body reminded me of an overfed baby, but there was nothing touching in the similarity.

"Don't be urbane, and don't stall. Stand up again."

He lay where he was, awkward and appalled. I took him by the collar and raised him to his feet. He stood swaying. The gauze bandage had come loose from his cheek and the wound was beginning to bleed.

"What do you want me to do?" he said. "I didn't kill your father."

I hardly heard him. Nothing that he could say meant anything, anyway. In a few hours I had learned to know him as well as if we had been intimate for years. The terrible figure who had cast his shadow across the city melted away in my hands to nothing much. An empty man bundled in layers of flesh—ruled, like an evil child, by cruel appetites and perverse little desires. The great body was loose with fear, sweating freely from every pore.

"Open the safe."

"I haven't got the combination," he said without conviction. "Rusty has it."

I struck his mouth with the back of my hand. Two narrow streams of blood trickled from its corners and beslobbered his chin. Tears formed in his large soft eyes.

"You can beat me," he said brokenly. "But I can't open the safe."

I struck his mouth again. The lower lip split like a plum that was rotten ripe. He put his hands over his face and moaned. Then he spread his palms in front of him, frowning miserably at the blood that smeared them. Two tears detached themselves from the inner corners of his eyes and glided down on either side of his nose.

"I can't," he said wildly. "I can't open it."

I struck his mouth again.

"I can't," he sobbed. "Leave me alone."

"I've been gentle with you, Kerch. But you haven't co-operated." I raised the automatic and clicked off the safety. "Now, you'll open it or I'll kill you. Hurry."

"I told you I can't," he whined.

"I won't wait any longer." I brought the gun to shoulder level and aimed it at his head.

He stared incredulously into the round hole through which death would come, too frightened to move. I saw the realization of death enter his eyes slowly. The realization that there would be no more Kerch, no more money to count and no soft small hands to count it, no more power and no will to power, no means of satisfying perverse desires and no more cruel appetites. No more Kerch.

He couldn't face the loss of himself. "Don't shoot," he said in a voice as thin as death. "I'll open it."

"Hurry."

I stood over him while his fingers cleared the dial. Ten. Twice around clockwise to fourteen. Counterclockwise passing thirty once, stopping on twenty-four. He pulled the heavy door open.

"Give me the papers that Mrs. Weather wanted."

"They don't matter now," he said. "She's dead."

I cuffed his left ear with my closed fist. "Don't argue, give them to me."

He opened a drawer in the upper right-hand corner of the safe, but I saw the gun before his hand could close on it, and hammered his knuckles with the muzzle of my gun. He lay down on the floor and rolled gently from side to side, crying to himself.

"You made a mistake. Get up and try again." I nudged his head with the toe of my boot. "Hurry."

He climbed to his knees and opened the next drawer. It was a filing drawer, containing tabbed cards in alphabetical order. He took a thick envelope from the back of the drawer and handed it to me. The name "Mrs. J.D. Weather" was typed across its face.

I pushed him out of the way and looked at the tabs in the drawer. The first name was unknown to me. The second name was Allister. The envelope behind it had "Mr. Freeman Allister" typed across its face.

Kerch was standing in the center of the room, bowed over his hurt hand. I sat behind his desk and set down my gun in front of me.

"Sit on the couch," I told him, and he did so.

Floraine Weather's envelope contained a marriage certificate, a newspaper clipping, and a notarized document giving her power of attorney, for all business and legal purposes, to one Roger Kerch. The marriage certificate stated that a woman named Floraine Wales had been married to a man named Roger Kerch in Portland, Oregon, on the 14th day of May, 1931. The headline of the clipping, which was from a Portland newspaper of the same day, was: "Vows Taken by Popular Young Couple." The story began: "In a charming private ceremony in the Baptist Church today, Miss Floraine Wales, daughter of Mr. and Mrs. Frederick Wales of Ventura, California, became the bride of Mr. Roger Kerch, son of Mr. and Mrs. Selby Kerch of Trenton, New Jersey. Both the bride and groom have been prominent for several years in local radio circles, the former Miss Wales having been secretary to the general manager, and Mr. Kerch, a well-known news commentator and program director. . . ."

There was a fairly clear picture of the two of them at the top of the page. Floraine looked young and pretty and virginal in her bridal veil, but she was recognizable. The man beside her, identified as Roger Kerch, did not look like the Kerch I knew. The young man in the morning coat who held her arm was lean and handsome, with romantic dark eyes and a flashing smile.

I glanced at the frog-faced man who was sitting on the couch sucking his knuckles, and then back at the picture. I could almost feel sorry for him, until I remembered the last time I had seen Floraine. Kerch had changed, but time and disease hadn't been too cruel to him.

I opened Freeman Allister's envelope, and laughed when I saw what it contained.

"My Dearest, Dearest Francie," the first letter began:

In the midst of an impossible situation, both political and domestic, my mind continually returns to you as the tired body of a runner leaps into a cool, sweet stream. How else could I continue to go on in this frightful town, condemned by law to live with the harridan out of hell who calls herself my wife, without the thought of you to support me and sustain me? Ah, to lie again between the clean white streams of your thighs, to rest my weary head upon your breast. This is my dream, waking and sleeping. Come you back from Chicago, my sister, my spouse, for my flesh and spirit are thirsting and hungering for you in a wide wasteland that offers no other comfort but you. . . .

The letter was signed: "Your own Freeman." It was dated March 23, 1944, when Freeman must have been quite a big boy.

"It didn't take much to scare Allister, did it?" I said to Kerch. "I suppose Sault stole these from his sister for you."

Kerch looked at me, and then at the door. The knob of the door was turning. I picked up the gun and crouched behind the desk.

"Be careful," Kerch shouted. "He's got a gun."

"Come out of there," said a voice I knew. "There are three of us, and we'll shoot to kill if you don't come out unarmed, with your hands up."

"Let him have it, Moffatt!" another man said. "He's a killer."

A pounding burst from a submachine gun stitched six holes across the door. The invisible bullets crossed the room high above my head like a flight of rapid insects.

"Stop it!" Kerch yelled. "I'm in here! Kerch!"

"It's all right, Mr. Kerch," Moffatt called. "We've got him. Now, you, are you coming out?"

I threw down my gun and stood up with my hands raised. "I'm coming," I said. "You can open the door."

Chapter 19

The room had a high ceiling and narrow windowless walls covered with burlap painted brown. A green-shaded droplight threw a bleak glare over the lower half of the room and cast the upper half into shadow. Beneath the light there was a tall desk of battered oak with a stool behind it. There was nothing else in the room but an old sour smell—the smell that men emit when they are dirty and afraid.

The aging police sergeant took my tie, my belt, my handkerchief, and my wallet. He didn't give me a receipt for them.

"We'll keep these for you," he said. "Looks as if we'll be keepin' them a long time."

I said: "Yeah."

The plain-clothes man Moffatt was standing in the hall when we went out.

"Guess we better put him in one of the new cells, eh?" the sergeant said.

"Bring him in under the light, Stan. He should be ready to talk."

"What do you want me to talk about?" I said. "Who stole my money last night?"

Moffatt hit me quickly on the side of the head. My arms jerked so that I involuntarily cut my wrists on the handcuffs.

"You telegraph your punches," I said. "You should stick to hitting people from behind."

He hit me with the edge of his hand on the back of my neck, just below the soft spot which his blackjack had made the night before. A buzzing sickness started in my head and ran erratically through my body, settling in my stomach and my knees.

171

"That's the way you want it, eh?" Moffatt said.

"Yeah," I said. "That's better." The sickness forced its way up my throat and I vomited on the floor.

"Better not hit him again," the sergeant said. "Not if you want him to be able to talk."

"Crap!" Moffatt said. "He deserves to be beaten to death. He's a brutal killer, Stan. All I can say is it's lucky for Mr. Kerch that Ron heard him call for help. Did you see what he did to poor Mr. Kerch?"

I said: "You mean, poor Mr. Kerch, the Christ of the Indian road?"

"Shut up, you. Or I'll use your face to clean up that mess you made on the floor."

"C'mon, Dave," the sergeant said. "You want to get his confession before Hanson gets back."

"Where the hell is Hanson, anyway?"

"Damned if I know. The Mayor took him off on some wild-goose chase. He's always getting crazy ideas."

They took me into a dark room and made me sit down on a backless chair. Moffatt turned on a bright light which shone directly into my eyes. I closed them, but found I couldn't do without that contact with the physical world. My mind was a blank wilderness, swept by a rattling wind of pain. I lost my balance and almost fell off the chair.

A fist came out of the darkness and cuffed me upright. "Open your eyes," Moffatt said. "Don't try playing possum."

I looked up at his shadowed face, then down his body at his dark wool tie, his solid vest front with the thin watch chain glittering across it, his thick legs planted apart in a bold, firm pose. He had an odor of sweat, cigars, bay rum, and after-shaving powder. I couldn't think of a word heavy enough to throw at him, so I said nothing.

"We know you killed Mrs. Weather," he said. "We know why. You'll save yourself a lot of trouble if you give us a statement."

"I like trouble."

The four fingers of his right hand ploughed down my

face from forehead to chin. I snapped at his hand, but
he drew it back too quickly.

"What big teeth you got, Grandmother," he said.
"You got too many teeth for good looks. Stan, give me
the knuckles."

The sergeant handed him a piece of molded brass,
which he slipped over his fingers. Then his armed fist
invaded my mouth. I felt a sharp piece of bone on my
tongue and spat it out between numb lips.

"You better not hit him again, Dave," the sergeant
said. "Judge Simeon don't like it when they're all
marked up."

"Don't worry, Stan. He was resisting an officer,
wasn't he? He tried to escape, didn't he?"

He drew back his dully shining fist. "You want to
dictate a statement while you still got the use of your
mouth?"

I leaned back and kicked him in the groin. He grunted and bent double, clutching at himself. "I'll kill
him," he said between gritting teeth. "The bastard ruptured me."

The sergeant's truncheon swung in a quarter circle to
my forehead, and a whirlpool of shattered light sucked
me down a drain and underground. Later, someone ex-
humed my consciousness—someone who said in a
blurred voice:

"I hope I ruptured you properly. Then you'll be the
last of the Moffatts."

Someone kicked a man who was lying on a floor.
Pity for the man on the floor coursed through my body
as real as pain. I'm learning some fine humanitarian
lessons, I thought, but somebody should put a stop to
this.

"Somebody should put a stop to this," the man on
the floor said. My tongue moved awkwardly in my
mouth and scratched itself on a broken tooth.

"So you'd resist an officer of the law in the performance of his duty," some clown said.

The man on the floor tried to get up but his stomach
was weak and the handcuffs interfered with the use of
his hands. I thought it would be nice if another whirl-

pool would take me down another drain, and immediately a whirlpool began to turn in my head. I lay back and waited for the blackout.

"Get up, get up," I said to the man on the floor. "You've got to get up and fight."

I opened my eyes and looked steadily at the leg of a table beside my head. Gradually it took on solidity, became realer than the whirlpool, realer than pain. From its reality I deduced the reality of my own body lying on the floor. My pity changed to anger and my head cleared.

I managed to sit up then, but a man standing over me planted his foot on my chest and flung me backwards. My very real head grazed the indubitable leg of the table. I rolled my head aside and lay quietly, fighting off self-pity. The repetition of physical violence, I told myself, is beginning to bore me. But boredom was another thing I had to fight.

A door opened and a ceiling light was switched on.

"What goes on here?" somebody said. "What do you think you're doing?"

"He tried to escape," Moffatt said. "He kicked me in the balls."

"You're not on duty, are you, Moffatt?"

"No, sir."

"Go home, then, before I lose my temper." I recognized the bitter, twanging voice of Inspector Hanson.

Moffatt went out and Hanson bent over me and looked into my face. "The bastard fixed you, didn't he!" He stepped behind me and helped me to my feet. I would have fallen again if he hadn't held me.

"Bring that chair over here, Sergeant," he said. "Then you can get out."

I sat down in the chair and he leaned against the table facing me. "I warned you last night, Weather. I told you you were heading into bad trouble."

"I'm doing all right," I said. "There's nothing the matter with me a good dentist can't fix."

"And a good lawyer?"

"Don't talk crap. The worst lawyer in the state could spring me from this kind of a frame-up. Who is the worst lawyer in the state, by the way? I'd like to talk to him."

"You want a lawyer?"

"Maybe I don't need one. Did you catch Garland?"

"He didn't run away very fast," Hanson said. "On account of he was dead."

"Dead?"

"You choked him, didn't you? When you cut off somebody's air supply it causes them to become dead."

"I didn't kill him."

"You were the one that was manhandling him, weren't you? You manhandled him a little too rough."

"I didn't choke him. I knocked him out. I broke his wrists so he couldn't shoot me. That's all."

"You're a rough boy, Weather. You seem to like hurting people."

"Whether I like it or not, sometimes it has to be done."

"Did it have to be done to Floraine Weather?" he barked.

"If you thought I killed her, you wouldn't be talking to me this way."

"What I think isn't here or there," he said. "I let the facts do the thinking for me."

"Facts can be arranged. Kerch murdered her. I saw him do it, and so did Garland and Rusty Jahnke. You've got three witnesses."

"One," he said sourly. "You don't count, and there isn't any Garland."

"What happened to Jahnke? I suppose you dropped him at some convenient street corner."

"He wasn't at the Wildwood. Maybe you have been having bad dreams? They say murderers have bad dreams."

"Go and find him, then. The city isn't paying you to sit in a room and make comical remarks."

He stood up and looked down at me with hot, green eyes. "Are you trying to tell me how to do my job?"

"It sounds like it. Climb off your high horse, Hanson, and be yourself. I think you've got the makings of a good cop. Allister seems to think so, too. Isn't it about time you did something about it? Your friend Kerch committed two murders last night—"

"Kerch is no friend of mine," he growled. "What do you mean, two murders?"

"Floraine Weather and Joe Sault. Maybe three: somebody killed Garland, and it wasn't me. Rusty Jahnke was his accomplice in both murders. If you're afraid to go after Kerch himself, you can bring in Rusty. You'll do it, Hanson, if the graft hasn't spread all the way down to the soles of your flat feet."

"Where did you get the idea you could give me orders?"

"As of today I'm paying part of your salary. I own property in this town, as of today, and I pay taxes. Does that make any sense to you? You've been taking lousy orders all your life. Take some decent orders for a change. Go and get Rusty Jahnke."

"I don't know where he is," he said uncertainly.

"You're afraid of Kerch," I taunted. "To hell with you, Hanson!—"

He slapped me across the face.

"To hell with you, Hanson!" I repeated. "Beat me up and toss me in a cell, you rotten, lily-livered grafter. I'll get the best lawyer in the state and tear this reeking town wide-open from gullet to gut. Get somebody to take me away, for Christ's sake. You stink in my nostrils, Hanson."

He trembled like an old hound after a long run. He didn't hit me again.

"Why don't you sock me some more, Hanson? There's no danger in it. I've got handcuffs on. Now Rusty Jahnke might take a shot at you, and scare the living daylights out of you."

"Shut your yap," he said. "I'm going to bring him in."

He walked stiffly towards the door, chewing his long lips.

"While you're at it, there's another witness against Kerch. You know Professor Salamander? You should be able to handle him, Inspector. He's very little and old."

He whirled on me savagely. "I said shut your yap! If you don't shut up, I'll shut you up for good!"

He turned again abruptly, and went out the door. The sergeant came back into the room, unlocked my handcuffs, and led me downstairs to the cells. I wasn't sorry when the iron door clanged shut. There was a wooden cot hinged to the concrete wall of my cell, and that was all I needed. I stretched out, found a section of my head that wasn't too sore to rest against the boards, and went to sleep.

A minute later—I found out afterwards it was more than an hour—I was wakened by a hand on my shoulder.

"What's the matter?" I said. "Are they attacking?" Then I remembered that it wasn't France or Germany, even though I was sleeping on wood, even though my whole body was stiff and sore.

"Wake up, Mr. Weather," the policeman said. "Mr. Sanford wants to see you."

"Tell him to go chase himself."

"Aw, come on now, Mr. Weather. You know you wouldn't want to talk like that to Mr. Sanford. He's waiting upstairs to see you."

I sat up carefully, balancing my head as delicately as if it were high explosive. My lips felt raw and puffed, and one of my broken teeth was aching viciously. "He can come down here."

"Come on, Mr. Weather. You wouldn't want to talk to him down here."

Alonzo Sanford was waiting in the room where Moffatt had questioned me.

"Here he is, Mr. Sanford," the guard said with forced enthusiasm. He went out and closed the door behind me.

"So good of you to return my call so soon," I said. "Please don't think me inhospitable if I fail to offer you a drink."

He walked towards me slowly, looking into my face. "Good God, John, what have they been doing to you? Your mouth—"

"Yeah, it makes me lisp a little, doesn't it? But I can still sound off."

"Who is responsible for this brutality?"

"You are, as much as anybody, I'd say. The man that used the brass knuckles on me doesn't matter. I'll take care of him myself one of these days—the way he needs to be taken care of."

"You must be hysterical, John. To claim that I have any responsibility—"

"Maybe I'm a little hysterical. Hysteria isn't such a bad thing. It makes you see things very clearly and simply, in black and white. You support a system in this town under which this kind of thing can happen to anybody—to anybody but you and your friends, that is. There are only two kinds of police systems, Sanford, when you look at it hysterically. The kind that exists to uphold the law and to treat everybody equally under the law, and the kind that exists to serve private interest. Your idea of a useful police force is the second kind—a police force that will lay off your friends and bear down hard on your enemies, a force of strike-breakers and bully boys, a Swiss Guard for the elite."

"You make it hard for me, John," the old man said, "but I do not consider you my enemy."

"That's not because I'm a man, is it? It's because I'm a property owner. You came over here this morning to talk property. Property has to stick together. The only reason you see the marks on my face is because it's got property behind it."

"Believe me, John, I sympathize with you. You've been violently mishandled, and it's only natural for you to be upset. Still, I fail to understand why you number me among your enemies. I came here to help you. You know that your father and I were close friends."

"No doubt you found him useful, as you hope to find me useful, perhaps?"

"He was closer to me than anyone." He spoke with the shallow sentimentality of the old.

"He was your political lieutenant, wasn't he? He built up the machine through which you kept the rubber workers in line and indirectly controlled the municipal government. I'm not concerned with personal blame—though I blame you both—but with the fact that the two of you saddled this town with a corrupt machine. The trouble is that corruption isn't something you can have a little of. It's like cancer; inject it into a political organism and it's bound to spread. It's almost an axiom that power that has been taken out of the hands of the people is bound to grow progressively more corrupt."

"You haven't seen as much of life as I have," Sanford said wearily. "Your picture is oversimplified and terribly one-sided. I admit that I've exercised political power in this city and state, and I've worked unceasingly to retain that power. But my motives have been purer than you suspect, I think. My industry is a small one, and it has not been easy to keep it from being swallowed up by its immense competitors. It has been my lifework to survive, so to speak, merely to keep my plants in operation. The Sanford plants are the economic heart of this city and of this whole area. If they were to close, as they are not going to do so long as I am alive, this city would become a ghost town. They would not be operating today if I had not deliberately developed my political power for the last fifty years. I'm not talking only of municipal politics, of course. But, if I lost political control of this city, I would have no weight at all in the state legislature, and very little influence in Washington."

"You wouldn't be able to survive, as you call it—by which you mean survive very comfortably, even luxuriously—if you gave political power back to the people?"

"If I had to pay union wages, if the city government got out of hand and raised my assessments and taxes, I wouldn't be able to survive."

"Isn't it possible, then, that you're an anachronism? You're trying to stay on top of the heap by forcing conditions to remain as you determined them fifty years ago."

"I have done what I have had to do," he said soberly. "My own hands are clean."

"Your picture is more oversimplified than mine, Mr.

Sanford. You've stayed on top of the heap and assumed that everything was fine because you were on top. Meanwhile, the heap rotted away from under you. I've been in some rotten towns, but never a rottener one than yours."

"Original sin, John. You can't change human nature. I've tried to set an example of decency in my own life."

"Don't go theological on me, and don't go self-righteous. You're the better half of a working partnership with the underworld. You're propped up by pimps, thieves, blackmailers, and murderers."

"Good morning, John. You can't expect me to remain here and listen to your wild nonsense."

He started around me towards the door, walking with the incontestable dignity of lifelong authority and wealth. I stood in his way.

"Just a minute," I said. "Let me tell you what's happened in this city in the last two years."

He stood still and regarded me coldly. I went on:

"You and my father built a machine to control the town. One pole of the axis was your wealth and social position, the other was my father's slot-machine graft and his influence with the ordinary people. Two years ago my father was shot, and you'd have expected the axis to bend a little. But that didn't happen, because the axis was more important than a man's life, or justice, or anything else at all. You took a new partner to hold up the other end of the axis, because you were old and tired and wouldn't dirty your own hands. The new partner was the very man who muscled in on my father and killed him—"

"That's not true," he said quickly. "It's merely another wild accusation."

"I intend to substantiate it. I've already substantiated some facts about your partner Kerch. Any power he has is based on blackmail. Surely you knew that he was blackmailing Floraine Weather? That the money you paid him for the Weather House undoubtedly went into his own pocket?"

"I knew nothing of the sort. Nor do I know it now."

"The evidence is in his safe at the Cathay Club.

Roger Kerch was married in 1931 to the woman who called herself Floraine Weather. Apparently they were never divorced. Floraine Weather was a bigamist, and Kerch got control of her property because he knew it. Did you?"

"Certainly not!"

"For all your knowledge of life, haven't you been rather naïve? Or was the situation too useful to you to be examined critically? It must have been useful, too, to have Kerch to control Allister for you, and through him, all the little people in the town who respect Allister and vote for him. Did you ever stop to wonder why Allister took orders from Kerch, and thus indirectly from you?"

"Allister never took orders from Kerch. The two men are violently antagonistic."

"Maybe so, but it never led to anything. Allister never took any sort of action against Kerch, and I'll tell you why. Kerch has something on him. Your partner has been blackmailing the Mayor of your city to keep him in line."

The old man walked to a chair and sat down heavily. His face showed neither shock nor confusion, but his eyes looked tired. "Leaving aside for the moment the validity of your accusations—they come as a complete surprise to me, but no doubt you have some reason for making them—I object to your calling this man my partner. I've had necessary business dealings with him, of course, as I have with practically every businessman in the state. But I have thoroughly detested the man from the first."

"You tolerated him and used him. In this town your mere tolerance of a man is like a stamp of approval. It makes him immune."

"If what you say of him is true, my tolerance will be withdrawn."

"I haven't told you all of it. He murdered Floraine Weather last night."

"Have you any evidence?"

"I have enough."

He said casually and dryly: "You didn't mention, by

the way, what Kerch has on Freeman Allister, as you put it. Surely our worthy reform mayor doesn't have a guilty secret?"

"It's going to stay a secret," I said. "It's strictly between Allister and himself."

He fluttered his hands in cold gaiety. "As you wish, John. You seem to have quite a talent, do you not, for discovering unsuspected skeletons in irreproachable closets? I've always considered Allister a veritable Cæsar's wife of political virtue."

The door of the room opened behind me and Allister came in. "Did I hear somebody taking my name in vain?" he said with strained cheerfulness. "Good morning, Mr. Sanford."

"Good morning, Freeman," he answered in an unruffled voice. "You know John Weather, don't you?"

"Yes, of course." He turned to me and his blue eyes widened. "Heavens, man, what happened to your face?"

"I bumped a door."

"Fortunately," Sanford said smoothly, "John's troubles are approximately at an end. I haven't had a chance to tell you, John, since we got off on that rather unrewarding discussion, but I've been talking to our Coroner, Dr. Bess, and he has established that Floraine Weather had been dead several hours before you were seen with her body. Something to which he referred as post-mortem lividity, I believe, indicates that her body had been moved after death. There also seemed to have been some attempt to give medical treatment to the wounds from which she bled to death. I presented those facts to Judge Simeon, and he was willing to set bail for you at $10,000. I took the liberty of posting your bail without consulting you."

"Thank you." I would have smiled if my mouth had been fit for it. "But I'll stay here until I can walk out without posting bail."

"Don't be ridiculous!" he said tartly. "It's merely a temporary loan. You have ample resources to cover it."

"I'll accept, if you realize clearly that I'm going to stay in this city and fight you."

"I realize that only too clearly." He smiled bitterly, got out of his chair with difficulty, and moved across the room. Before he went out he turned his white head on his scrawny bird's neck and gave me a long look: "I warn you, however, that the possession of property in a so-called democracy involves more complex responsibilities than you realize."

"Yeah," I said. "Some of us did a lot of thinking and talking about those things when we were in the army. Human decency has its responsibilities, too. And I don't like the implications in your phrase 'so-called democracy.'" The closing door put a period to my sentence, but I had a feeling that my argument with Alonzo Sanford would go on till he died.

Allister had gone to the window and raised the blind while we talked, and stood restlessly looking out at a wall of grimy white brick.

"Hanson gave me the word on Garland," I said when he turned.

"That he died, you mean?"

"Yeah, he thought I killed him. If Garland had died of a fractured skull, I might blame myself. Or congratulate myself. But he was choked to death, Hanson said."

"And you didn't choke him?" There was a queer look in his cloudy blue eyes, which probably meant that he didn't believe me.

"I could have, but I didn't. I just put him out of action, the quickest way I knew how. I never killed a man except when I was wearing a uniform, and that made it all right and proper."

"It must have been Kerch," Allister said slowly. "He would naturally destroy the witnesses against him."

"Did he go out to the Wildwood again?"

"He must have. Rusty Jahnke was in his suite at the Palace. That old quack doctor Salamander was working on him there when Hanson picked him up."

"Hanson really did it, then?"

"Yes. He's bringing Rusty and Salamander here for questioning."

"If you're in on all this, aren't you taking a chance?"

He walked diagonally across the room with a jerky, forward-leaning stride, and came to an unstable position of rest against the wall. "What do you mean?" he said. "Hanson is handling the case."

"But you're backing him up, aren't you?"

"I can't act openly." He moved sideways against the wall as if the room cramped him, as if any four walls threatened his freedom. "I have cogent reasons."

"I opened Kerch's safe this morning."

He looked at me with such startled eyes that I might have been in command of a firing squad and about to give the final order. "Yes?" he said.

"No doubt you think Kerch can ruin your political career. I doubt it. If you act quickly and boldly and pin the murders on him, he won't be able to do a thing to you. Your affair with Mrs. Sontag is small potatoes compared with the things we have on Kerch. But you've got to take the bit in your teeth and act now, or he'll take the play away from you."

There was fear and confusion in his eyes, as if he suspected me of bitter irony. "What did you see in Kerch's safe?"

"Your letters to Mrs. Sontag. I think you were a fool to let him frighten you with those. If you'd have the courage of your indiscretions, you could fight him in the open and win."

"You don't understand this town. I'd lose the support of the one group of people I can count on."

"All right." I sat down and looked out of the window. The dirty brick wall which cut off the horizon was as blank and stubborn as human fear. "I'm bloody tired of giving pep talks. I've given so many pep talks in the last two years that I feel like sealing off my mouth and stopping talking for good."

"I don't know what to do," he said miserably.

I stood up and gave him the pay-off: "If you've got any guts left at all, you can make a monkey out of Kerch. Have you got a gun?"

"Yes, I got one from Hanson before we went out to the inn."

"Then go out to the Cathay Club and bring in Kerch."

"I'm not a gunman."

"Neither is he."

"But what about my letters in his safe? You haven't got them, have you?"

"No, they're probably still there. But I think I can remember the combination."

"You can?"

"Lend me your pen and an envelope."

He gave me writing materials and I sat down at the desk. My head wasn't good for much else by then, but it was still a good head for figures. One by one I picked the numbers out of my bruised memory and set them in the right order.

"It's an envelope in the second drawer from the upper right-hand corner," I said. "Alphabetically, under 'A.' Kerch is a great man for system."

He thanked me emotionally when I handed him the combination. Then he went out the door in nervous haste, like a rattled hunting dog going up for his last chance to pass the test on the firing range.

Chapter 20

The sergeant opened the door and moved backwards into the room. "Bring him in here, Alec," he said. "Inspector Hanson wants him in here."

He looked taken aback when he turned and saw me sitting there. "You're free to go now, Mr. Weather. I'll take you out to the desk so you can check out."

"I feel too weak to move."

"Hold it a minute, Alec," the sergeant called into the hall. He turned to me again with a look that tried to be ingratiating and wasn't. "You can't sit here, Mr. Weather. Mr. Sanford bailed you out, didn't you know?"

"I like it here. It's very interesting."

An obscure worry crawled across his face. "I didn't want to hit you, Mr. Weather, you know that. I tried my best to keep Moffatt from beating you up. You won't say anything to Inspector Hanson?"

"I've got nothing against you but your job and your personality and the company you keep. I won't tattle on you. But you better keep out of dark alleys for a while. And tell your pal Moffatt to keep off the streets entirely."

"Yeah, sure, Mr. Weather. Don't you think you need some first aid for your face? Come with me and I'll get you fixed up."

"I'm staying here. You can bring me my belt and tie—and my wallet, with all the money in it."

"O.K., Mr. Weather. But the Inspector don't want you here when he's questioning a prisoner." He plodded out.

A minute later Hanson came in, with Rusty Jahnke handcuffed and escorted by a uniformed policeman.

186

Jahnke looked beaten and sick, the way I felt. His face was badly bruised and his head hung down on his chest. The unbruised sections of his face were as pale and inert as lard. Even when he looked up under his red brows and saw me, there was hardly a flicker of recognition in his small eyes.

Hanson gave me a hard, bright look as if to say: "You see?" He carried his body with authority.

"Do you mind if I sit in on this, Inspector? If Jahnke starts telling his dreams, I'm an expert on dreams."

"Yes, you stay, Weather," he said crisply. "Sit him under the light, Alec, and pull down the blind. I told Rourke to hold the other one across the hall."

Alec pushed Jahnke into the chair and sat down behind him with a pencil and stenographic notebook. Under the staring light the red spikes of Jahnke's beard stood out individually and cast minute shadows on his chin. "If you think you can get anything outa me," he said, "you're nuts. I wanta lawyer. I wanta talk to Mr. Kerch."

"You'll get a lawyer," Hanson snapped. "And you'll get Mr. Kerch. I'll put you in adjoining cells."

Jahnke uttered a loose and mirthless laugh. "You're talking awful big, copper. Pretty soon you'll be talking awful small."

"I don't care how you talk, Jahnke, so long as you talk. At what time did your employer cut Mrs. Weather to death? Was it before or after he beat Sault to death?"

Jahnke looked up in stupid surprise. Perhaps he didn't know Floraine was dead. More likely he hadn't expected to be asked such large questions so definitely and so soon.

"I don't know nothing about it. Somebody hit me from behind and knocked me out, and I didn't see nothing happen to nobody."

"You held Sault's arms while Kerch beat him," I said. "I saw you."

Hanson turned on me. "When I want you to talk up, I'll ask you to."

This encouraged Jahnke: "He's a dirty liar," he yelled. "He killed Sault and buried him himself."

"How could you know?" Hanson said. "You were unconscious."

"Somebody told me. Mr. Kerch told me."

"Was Mr. Kerch there when Sault was killed?"

"No, he wasn't there. Nobody was there except this guy here. He did it." He started to raise a hand to point at me, but his handcuffs thwarted the gesture.

"How do you know he did it?"

"I told you Mr. Kerch told me."

"But he wasn't there."

"No, but Sault was a friend of his, and he heard about it."

"I'll tell you how close friends they were," Hanson said in a hard voice. "Sault was beaten to death with an iron spocn. It's got his hair and his blood type on it, and it's got Kerch's fingerprints."

"You're bluffing, copper," Jahnke feebly scoffed. "You ain't got Kerch's fingerprints."

"But I have. He left them all over his suite in the Palace. He was too careless to get away with murder. He thought he had nothing to worry about, so he didn't even take elementary precautions. That's why we're going to burn him, Jahnke. And that's why you're in so deep I can hardly see the top of your thick head."

"You ain't got nothing on me."

Hanson laughed in his face. "You've got a faint chance of getting off with life, Jahnke. I've already given it to you. But you're not talking the way you should be. You're not talking about the murder of Floraine Weather."

Jahnke's head was down on his chest again like a tiring bull's. "I don't do no talking till I see a lawyer. You can't make me talk."

"All right, Alec, take him away. I'd rather get it from Salamander, anyway, he's got more brains." He turned to me and said in a conversational tone: "If we don't get him for killing Sault, we've got him for the murder of your father." His eyelid slid over his eye and snapped open again.

"You can't frame me for old man Weather," Rusty said to his back. "I wasn't even there."

Hanson turned on him again, and barked: "You were seen driving a car in the neighborhood of the Mack Building at the time of the shooting. I've got a witness, Jahnke."

"That wouldn't prove nothing, even if it was true. There was plenty of cars on the street—" He stopped with his mouth open.

"I suppose your employer Mr. Kerch told you that, too?"

"I didn't say nothing about Mr. Kerch. He didn't have nothing to do with it."

"Maybe you can tell me who did. You were there. You saw all those cars on the street."

"There's always lots of cars on the street that time of night."

"What time, Jahnke? What time exactly? What time in the evening of April 3, 1944, did you shoot and kill J.D. Weather?"

"I didn't kill him, I tell you. I didn't even know about it till afterwards. Ask Garland, he'll tell you I didn't know about it."

"You want me to get in touch with Garland's spirit?"

"What are you trying to pull on me? Just call up Garland and ask him. He'll tell you I didn't know about it."

"I haven't a telephone that would do it," Hanson said cheerfully. "Garland's dead."

"You're a liar. You're bluffing me again. You can't bluff me."

"You want to come over to the morgue and see him? You want to poke your fingers in his eyeballs?"

"Garland in the morgue? I don't believe it."

"Everybody dies some time, Jahnke. They die like flies in your racket. Why should I try to kid you? You'll read it in the papers—if they give you any papers in the death house."

Jahnke's pale-blue eyes looked up into the light and were stared down.

"If Garland's dead, then I can tell you," he said finally. "He's the one that killed old man Weather."

"That's an easy way out, isn't it, Jahnke? Putting the blame on a dead man?" Hanson paused, and then rapped out: "Now let's have the truth!"

"I'm telling you the truth. Garland killed him."

"Where's your proof?"

"The proof is what I saw."

"You just said you weren't there."

"I wasn't there when it happened, but I was right before. That musta been when somebody saw me in the car."

"Whose car?"

The clumsy evasion of his brain showed on his face. "Garland's car. I was driving for Garland."

"And who did Garland work for? Who hired him to kill J.D. Weather?"

"Nobody. I don't know nothing about that. I told you I didn't even know he killed Weather till after."

"But why would Garland kill J.D. Weather? He didn't even know him, did he?"

"No, he didn't know him, except to see."

"Who hired him?"

"I don't know. I don't want to talk about that. I told you I'd tell you what I saw."

"Go ahead. What did you see?"

"Garland and me was tailing Weather. We been tailing him off and on for a week. We was brought here from Chicago, and that was the job I was hired for, to tail J.D. Weather."

"Who hired you?"

"You know who I work for. I only worked for one boss in this town. The same guy that's gonna take your badge off your chest and pin it to your tail."

"Sure, sure," Hanson said sardonically. "After you get through talking, we'll have a cup of tea and you can read my teacup for me. That's after you get through talking."

"Who's been buying you, Hanson?" He tried again to look up into Hanson's face but the light was too strong.

"Stop worrying about me and get on with your story. Kerch ordered you to follow Weather and wait for a chance to kill him—which you did."

"He didn't give me any orders like that. I took my orders from Garland. I was just driving the car. I wasn't even packing a rod. That's the truth. You can ask anybody."

"There isn't anybody to ask."

"Anyway, I wasn't in on any shooting. I guess Garland had been figuring the best place to shoot him and make a getaway, and decided that the Mack Building was a good place. Old man Weather used to pass there every night about the same time. This was about half past six and we was double-parked near the corner, waiting for him to go past. Garland was sitting beside me in the front seat. I guess he was casing the second-story windows but I didn't know what he was doing. All of a sudden he jumped out and told me to drive around the corner and beat it, he'd take a taxi back to the hotel. He ran in the Mack Street entrance of the Mack Building and I drove away. When I was halfway down the block I heard the two shots but I kept right on going. I didn't know who did the shooting or who got it until I read in the night papers that it was J.D. Weather."

"What did you do then?"

"What would anybody do? I kept my mouth shut."

"Did you talk to Garland about it?"

"I never talked to Garland about nothing. I took orders from him. I told you everything I saw and everything I did, and that's all I can tell you."

"It's not a very good story, Jahnke. You should've been able to do better than that to save your skin. Didn't you help Garland jimmy the door in the Mack Building? Didn't you stand by in the car to give him a quick out?"

"I'm telling you the truth. I didn't tell you nothing else but the truth. Garland didn't want me around, see? He didn't want no witnesses."

"Your stories are bad, but they're getting better. Let's hear what you can do on Mrs. Weather now."

"I ain't saying no more. When I tell you the truth it don't do me no good. It don't do me no good no matter what I say." His jaw set stolidly and his mouth clamped shut.

"Take him down to the cells, Alec," Hanson said briskly. "There's nobody in nine, is there? And you better get Dr. Brush to look at his head. We wouldn't want a fine intelligent witness like Jahnke to die on our hands, would we? Although it might save electricity."

"——you, you ——ing ——," Jahnke said repetitiously as he was led out.

Hanson turned to me, rubbing his hands. His green eyes shone in the margin of the white glare like sunlight caught in the bottom of a beer bottle. "You asked me a question last night, Weather. Now it's answered."

"I've got to take back what I said, Inspector. When somebody knocks the chocks out from under you, you're hell on wheels."

"All I needed was something on Kerch. You gave it to me."

"But you had a witness who saw Jahnke near the Mack Building on the night of the murder. You didn't tell me that last night."

"It didn't mean anything last night. There were hundreds of people on the streets, and Jahnke was one of them. If I had been able to follow it up two years ago—"

"What stopped you?"

"Politics," Hanson said. "I was ordered to lay off Kerch and his little family."

"By whom?"

"You want him in here, Inspector?" somebody said from the door.

"Yeah, bring him in." He said to me: "We'll talk about it later."

"But you believe Jahnke's story?"

"Sure," he said. "He hasn't got enough brains to make a story that good. And if somebody taught it to him two years ago, he'd have forgotten the words and music by now."

The sergeant crossed the room and silently handed

me my belt and tie and wallet. The bills in the wallet were folded. I never fold bills in a wallet.

"Thank you," I said.

"Don't mention it, Mr. Weather."

On his way out, the sergeant passed Salamander and the policeman who was bringing him in. A caricaturist who wanted to portray the degradation of age and fear, but who had run out of colors and had nothing but a lump of dirty yellow wax to work with, might have made the face that Salamander carried sideways on his neck. The glance of his urine-yellow eyes darted into every dark corner of the room, like a frenzied rodent looking for a hole. He saw me but avoided my eyes.

"This is a despicable outrage," his large voice said. But the movements of his thin, old body were infinitely humble as he crossed the room in a slow lope on continuously bent knees.

"Don't start telling me how Kerch is going to take care of you, Professor. Kerch is going to be too busy taking care of himself. How come you're a professor, by the way? Professor of what? Professor of abortion?"

The waxen face was so bloodless and transparent under the light that you could see the shadow of the skull. "Professor of Occult Sciences," he said apologetically.

"You don't practice medicine any more, eh?"

"I retired from the profession some years ago."

"I'm not talking about illegal operations. We'll forget about that for now. Have you been doing any surgical work lately?"

"As you know very well, I was examining Mr. Jahnke's head when you burst in on us. I wouldn't describe that as surgical work. I was merely doing a favor for a friend as one layman to another, you understand. I warn you, however, that he requires medical attention, since he probably had a slight concussion."

"He's getting it. But apart from Jahnke, you haven't been giving medical treatment to anyone lately?"

"Certainly not," the old man said. "I reiterate that I am no longer a member of the medical profession. For many years I have been concerned exclusively with the spiritual ills of mankind."

"Uh-huh. Weather, have you ever seen this specimen before?"

"I saw him working on Mrs. Weather at the Wildwood Inn. I heard him tell Kerch he couldn't save her."

"He's a liar!" Salamander cried shrilly. "You're trying to frame me!"

"That's what they all say. But I go by the facts myself. The facts don't lie, if you study them carefully enough. How many stitches did you put in her face and neck?"

"I don't know what you're talking about."

"Come off it, Professor. We've got the marks of the stitches on Mrs. Weather. We've got the bloody pieces of catgut you put in your garbage this morning. We've got a direct witness. What else do you want—Technicolor movies of the big operating scene?"

Salamander's face and body seemed to shrink perceptibly, and became very still. Only the clean, thin hands moved in his lap. They scampered lightly and aimlessly, like blind, white spiders, up and down his fleshless thighs.

"I could never refuse to minister to the afflicted," he said at last. "Mrs. Weather was my employer, in a sense. When I was informed that she had been seriously injured in an accident, I did what I could for her. When she died in spite of my efforts, I removed the stitches in order to protect myself against prosecution as an unlicensed practitioner."

"Who informed you of the accident? Who took you to the Wildwood?"

"Mr. Roger Kerch."

"That's fine," Hanson said. "Take him down and put him in one of the new cells, Ron. We'll take his full story later."

"I want a lawyer," the old man said as he was led out. "Don't think I can't afford to pay a good lawyer."

"Get him a lawyer if he wants one," Hanson said. "Get everybody a lawyer—they're going to need one. We're booking him for now as a material witness."

"Are you ready to bring in Kerch?" I said.

"Right." He took a heavy automatic out of his shoulder holster, examined the clip, and replaced it.

"Let's go."

"You better stay here and see Dr. Brush—"

"Let's go," I said again. "If I don't ride with you I'll follow you in a taxi."

He shrugged his high shoulders and put on his hat. I had slipped my belt on but I couldn't be bothered with a tie, so I stuffed it in my pocket.

On the way out he said: "Don't you ever get tired?"

"Kerch stimulates me," I replied. "The way I feel about him is like benzedrine."

We drove straight west on a boulevard that was parallel to Main Street and almost clear of traffic.

"We've got enough on Kerch to fry him twice over," Hanson said. "But there are some things I still don't understand. Sure, he came to town with a couple of hired gunmen to kill your father and muscle in on his slot-machine rac— business. But how in hell did he get Floraine Weather to co-operate with him? She didn't have to let him take over the Cathay Club, for one thing. What do you think, was she working for Kerch all along? Did he send her here in the first place to marry J.D. if she could, and make an opening for him?"

"I doubt it. We can't be sure, but she didn't talk that way. I think she came to town with my father and married him because he had money and was getting old. Kerch heard about the marriage and followed her here. He studied the setup a little and it gave him a brilliant idea. You see, Floraine married Kerch a long time ago and never took the trouble to get a divorce. Probably he dropped out of her life completely for a good many years, and she practically forgot about him. Then he came to town."

"I get it—blackmail." He glanced quickly to left and right and went through a red light at fifty. "Now, why would a woman with her figure marry a thing like that?"

"He didn't always look like that. I think that's the

real reason he cut her. It didn't do him any good at all."

"Killing the goose that laid the golden eggs, eh?"

"Exactly. That's why he hired Garland to kill my father, so Floraine would be able to start laying golden eggs for him. It'd have been better for her in the long run if she'd come to you and told her story two years ago. I don't think she had a very happy two years."

"I guess not," Hanson said soberly. "But I told you I had orders to lay off Kerch."

"You didn't tell me who gave them to you."

"The Chief did, but it wasn't his idea. He takes orders from the police board. I figured it was the new mayor, but I couldn't figure why. Allister campaigned on a reform platform and claimed he was going to clean up the rackets. He said he was going to run your father out of town. Then, as soon as he gets in, less than a week after your father died, he starts fronting for a rat like Kerch."

"Kerch was blackmailing him, too."

"He was? What with?"

"That's not your business."

"Maybe you know what you're talking about, but it doesn't look like it. If Allister wasn't backing me now, I wouldn't be able to do what I'm doing."

"Things have changed," I said. "Forget what I told you about Allister. He's all right."

"One thing—I don't think he has to worry about anything Kerch can do to him. Kerch is a gone gosling."

He turned sharply right at the next traffic light, came onto the highway at the city limits, and turned left again towards the Cathay Club. "Come Again," a painted tin sign at the side of the road said. "We Hope You Have Enjoyed Your Stay."

Hanson parked in the club's driveway and walked quickly to the back door with me at his heels. The back door was unlocked and he went in, gun first. The door of the office was open and the lights were burning. Kerch sat behind the desk with his battered head sagging forward and his eyes closed. The dark little Cyclops eye in the center of his forehead gave him a queerly alert expression.

But the expression on Kerch's face no longer mattered to me. What mattered was the girl lying on the floor beside the leather couch, her clean cotton dress soiled by a red stain that spread downward across her left breast. I had been seeing a good deal of blood, but I had never fully realized what a waste it was to let blood run out of a body. The thought that she might be dead broke in my mind like a cold wave and brought me to my knees beside her. She was still breathing.

"Call an ambulance, Hanson. Tell them to come fast."

"Yeah." He picked up the phone on the desk, and used it.

I tore the dress down from her left shoulder. I didn't like to bare her breast in front of him, but it was necessary.

He put down the phone and squatted beside her. "Don't look too bad to me. Too high to get the lung, unless it was deflected. Looks as if it broke the collarbone, but that ain't so bad."

"Ambulance coming?"

"Right away."

"See that they take good care of her, will you?"

"She's a witness, isn't she?" He had taken a large clean handkerchief out of his pocket, and was folding it lengthwise. He looked at me over his shoulder with narrowed eyes. "Say, this Kaufman girl a friend of yours?"

"More than that. If I hadn't brought her out here, this wouldn't have happened."

"What the hell did happen? You think Kerch shot her and committed suicide? No, that don't make sense. No burns on his face, no gun. What was *she* doing here?"

"She drove me out this morning. After Moffatt got me, I guess she was afraid to come downstairs. Then she heard the shot that killed Kerch, and came down anyway. She must have recognized the man that did it."

"Or woman."

"That's a heavy-caliber wound. Women don't pack forty-fives."

"They don't, eh?" He had finished his temporary dressing of the wound and stood up. "But we'll call it a man. It doesn't follow that she knew him."

"Maybe not, but she does." And so did I.

"Who?"

"The man that did this. Lend me your gun."

"I can't do that, Weather. Strikes me you're over-eager. Who you want to gun for?"

"You wouldn't believe me if I told you, and there's no time to argue. I'll take him with my bare hands. But a gun's more certain."

"A gun's too certain. Five dead are enough."

I started for the door.

"You better stay here with me, boy."

"To hell with you!" I left him with the unconscious girl. I wanted to stay with her myself, but there was one person in the city who interested me more just then. Her car was still parked behind the Cathay Club, and the keys were in it. I got in and headed for the Harvey Apartments. I didn't pull in to the curb for the ambulance that passed me screaming west.

Chapter 21

The voices I could hear through the thin door of Francie Sontag's apartment told me that I was in time.

"I won't keep quiet!" her bitter voice was saying. It was like a key speech in a play I had heard before. "You can't make me."

"But you must," the man said. "You're making too much noise now. Somebody might hear you."

"I want everybody in town to hear me."

"Be quiet." His voice was small and tight. "You're hysterical. You're forgetting that you're in this as deep as I am."

"Oh no, I'm not. I never knew what went on. You didn't even tell me they were killing my own brother last night."

"I didn't know—"

"You sat on your bony rear and let them kill him. You wanted him dead, didn't you?"

"Listen to me, Francie." The grim patience in his voice was wearing thin. "How could I know it was Joey?"

"You could've gone to the Wildwood when this boy called you. You were Joey's last chance, and you didn't lift a finger to help him." Her voice had begun to rise and fall in a gasping rhythm.

"I had nothing to do with it. He meddled with things that were too big for him, and they killed him. Anyway, what's a gorilla like him compared with you and me?"

"Mr. Fine-Gentleman Allister!" she cried viciously. "You got your gall talking about gorillas. His little finger was worth five of you. He was a man, and he didn't drool at the mouth with words. I'd rather hear him say

199

hello to me again than listen to you jabbering all night."

"I thought you loved me." Allister's voice was softened by a dangerously unstable humility which could change suddenly to anything at all. "You always said you loved me."

"I was crazy, wasn't I? How could I love a murdering hypocrite like you? But I'm not crazy any more."

"Maybe you're crazy today for the first time." His voice was dead and monotonous now. "You're the only one left who knows about me."

"Kerch knows. Garland knows."

"Kerch and Garland are dead. You're the only one left alive, Francie."

"You killed them?" Her voice had lost its scornful stridency and had become little and tinny with fear. "I don't believe it."

"Believe what you like. I've given you your chance and you have failed me. Everyone has failed me." His voice vibrated with an unnatural timbre, as if he was approaching the emotional level where murder would be possible again.

I tried the door. It was locked. The doorknob rattled slightly when I removed my hand from it.

"What was that?" he said.

I stepped back across the hallway and took the lock away with my left shoulder. They were facing each other in the middle of the room, in stiff attitudes, like children caught at forbidden play. He turned on me with his hand in his coat pocket, his face and his whole body fumbling for his gun. Before I reached him the woman stepped behind him and seized his arms. He struggled in her grip, but she was a big woman and her hold was strong. She got the gun and he stopped struggling.

He tried to organize his face in a smile, as if they were playing games together. "Hello, Weather," he said without conviction.

I didn't like to go near him. I had a notion that his tense body would be giving off a sour-sweat odor of depravity. But I moved close up to the wretched smile and took the envelope from his breast pocket. He winced and jerked as if I was trying to tickle him. I had an impulse to hit him then, but I held it back. Violence might destroy the remnants of human dignity that kept him erect and smiling, and turn him into something queer—so queer that I wouldn't want to look at it. Another violence might do something to me, too—make me howl like a dog or cry like a baby or plait daisies in my hair.

The woman stepped back from us both, with the heavy automatic in her hand. The long minutes with Allister had given her skin a greenish patina of fear, and her eyes had a belladonna stare.

"You better go out in the kitchen and get a drink of water," I said.

She looked questioningly at the gun in her hand.

"Don't worry. I can handle him."

I never saw a convict walk off the scaffold when the trap failed to work, but she showed me how they walk. With slow, incredulous steps, and a backward glance at death.

I opened the envelope with Allister's name on its face. He moved suddenly to snatch it from me, but with only half his heart. I thrust him back with the flat of my hand. He lay down on the chesterfield with one knee dragging on the floor and his face hidden.

Nearly all the letters in the bulky envelope were addressed to Francie Sontag at a Chicago hotel. March 24, 1944—"Francie My Dear One: Your letter was very sweet. . . ." March 25, 1944—"My Sweet Love: I lay awake for hours thinking. . . ." March 26—"Darling Francie: Today is the birthday of our love. One year ago today. . . ." March 27—"Flesh of My Flesh . . ." March 29—"My Only Love. . . ."

The last letter, typed in duplicate on heavy bond paper, was addressed to Judge Ernest Simeon. Both copies were signed "Freeman Allister," but neither was dated. "Dear Judge Simeon," it began.

I can no longer live with the memory of the crime I have committed, the knowledge of the great wrong

I have done. I write this in haste, but in deep sincerity, to make whatever amends I can to the society whose most sacred law I have broken. I ask not for mercy, but only for justice. It is no excuse for my crime, nor do I offer it as such, that I was the creature of an overweening ambition and a criminal pride that distorted my moral vision.

But enough of such hesitations. This is a confession rather than an apologia. On the evening of April 3, I shot and killed J.D. Weather of this city. The murder was committed from the second-story window of a disused office in the Mack Building. It was a premeditated crime, planned and prepared for in advance. After its commission I disposed of my weapon, a Smith and Wesson revolver, in a sewer on Mack Street. I then went to my parked car and drove home. Mr. Weather was an obstacle to my political advancement and my motive for killing him was political ambition.

I write to you now because I can no longer bear the burden of my conscience. I wish to be tried and punished for my crime. Only then will my soul find peace.

Try not to think too hardly of an old friend.

Before I finished the letter, Mrs. Sontag came out of the kitchen. She moved hesitantly like a visitor in a sickroom and seemed surprised by the tranquillity of the atmosphere.

"What are you going to do with him? Aren't you going to call the cops?"

I put the letters on the table behind me. "Are you in a hurry?"

"He was going to kill me, wasn't he? I spend three years massaging his personality, trying to build him up into some kind of a man, and he ends up trying to kill me." She seemed to be spitting the words at the inert man on the chesterfield.

"I'll get around to calling the police. It says in the letter that he wants to be tried and punished for his crime."

"All right. I was just wondering. I can wait." She screwed a cigarette into a long red holder, lit it with a table lighter, and sat down in a dim corner of the room. Her color had improved, but she was still looking a little faded. She gulped hard on the cigarette.

Allister sat up and faced me. "I wrote that letter under duress. It will never be admitted in evidence. I wrote it from dictation on my typewriter and signed it at the point of a gun."

"It sounds quite a bit like you. Maybe you and Kerch have similar styles, at that. You both use words without any real feeling for what they mean."

"That letter is worthless to you. As a lawyer, I know what I'm talking about." He spoke with authority and I was surprised at his comeback. I wondered what he had done to himself while he lay with his face turned away.

"You killed to get this letter," I said. "Backed by Mrs. Sontag's testimony, it will do you a lot of harm. And the bullet in Kerch's head is going to correspond with the rifling on the gun you used."

His answer was glib. "I performed a public service in shooting Kerch. He resisted arrest, and, as chief magistrate of this city, it is my duty to enforce the law."

"Was Garland resisting arrest when you strangled him—unconsciously resisting arrest?"

"You have no evidence that I killed Garland. You have no usable evidence against me at all. Francie will never testify against me. If she tried to, her evidence could be invalidated on moral grounds."

"Moral grounds!" she yelled from her corner. "There's only one thing in my life I'm ashamed of, and that's you. I'll sing you into the chair, Mr. Morality."

The superficial calm of his face cracked wide-open and let his teeth show. "If I go, you'll go with me. You can't talk about me without convicting yourself as an accessory."

"Because I knew you got that revolver from Joey? Don't kid me!"

"Maybe you should study the tabloids, Allister. Any jury will recognize her right to protect her brother, at least to refrain from handing him over to the police. Especially now that he's dead."

He adopted another mood, with the speed of a quick-change artist and the same effect of artificiality. "Look, Weather, the woman doesn't matter. She won't do anything by herself. Now I understand you intend to stay here, and take over your father's interests—"

"No sale. I'm going to run them clean."

"Of course." He shifted again. "That's what I mean. If my name is dragged in the dirt, municipal reform will suffer an irreparable setback. Last night we agreed to work together, John."

"Don't call me John."

"Sorry. I've done wrong, I admit that. But it was my means that were at fault, not my ends. I killed your father—it's a terrible thing to have to say, isn't it?—but I did it because I sincerely believed that it was for the general good. I have sincerely regretted my crime, as that letter proves—"

"You wrote it at the point of a gun."

"Please let me finish. I have learned my lesson, Weather. I have learned that ends must never be subordinated to means, because the ends come to be determined by the means. Can't we still work together for a good purpose?"

He spoke clearly and rapidly, enunciating his phrases with athletic movements of his mouth and nostrils. They meant no more to me than words read in alphabetical order out of a dictionary.

"Save your eloquence for the jury," I said. "In a few minutes you'll be believing that story. That's why your type is so dangerous, Allister. You can make yourself believe anything."

"I told you I've seen my mistakes—"

"Listen to me for a change. You identify yourself with a cause, and all that means is that your ambition acquires a flavor of sanctity. You can convince yourself that you're working for a higher purpose, a purpose so high that it places you above the law. You kill a man, but you're not a murderer. You're a political assassin killing in the interests of good government with you at the head of it."

"You've got him pat," the woman said. "When he does it, he thinks it doesn't stink."

"Do I have to sit here and listen to her recriminations?"

"Tie a can to it, Mr. Allister-Pallister. You can't go to bed with a woman without pretending that you're kneeling at the altar in a bloody church."

His body jerked towards her. "You'd throw filth on every dream I ever had."

"Filth!" she spat. "*You* filth!" The gun moved slightly in her hand, and for a moment the room stopped breathing and became as silent as eternity.

"Maybe you'd better go out in the kitchen again," I said. "We've got things to talk about."

"I got a right to be here, haven't I? It's my house."

"Go out in the kitchen. And you'd better give me that gun."

"No you don't. I'm hanging on to this." She got up slowly and walked out of the room with a contemptuous weaving of her hips.

"That's what you get for trying to kill people," I said. "She doesn't like you any more."

He turned and watched her through the doorway, as she sat down in a kitchen chair and laid the gun on the table in front of her. When he spoke again, it was in a hushed and altered voice. "It seems impossible," he said, "that I should try to kill anyone. And I've killed three. It isn't any use, is it?"

"Murder?"

"Murder, or anything. I'm finished. I was finished four years ago, if I'd only known it. I should have killed myself then, and been done with it."

"What happened four years ago?"

He looked up and tried to smile, but his face wouldn't function properly. "I can't even be sure of that. You wouldn't understand if I tried to tell you. I suppose it was the war."

"We've all been in a war."

"I wasn't. I didn't get in, and that's the point. I tried for a commission after Pearl Harbor, but I couldn't pass the medical. They classified me as a psychoneurotic. Then my wife cut me off."

"Skip it."

"But it's important. She has weird ideas of heredity, and she said she wouldn't take the risk of bearing me any children. We'd only been married two years—I married late—and I loved my wife."

"But you don't any more?"

"I don't love anyone," the empty voice said. "Least of all, myself. You'd never believe what I used to be, Weather. I was a good man according to my lights. I believed in truth and justice, and I fought for those things, by God!" But the words came out with an unreal accent, like fragments of a language he had almost forgotten. "For ten years I fought for them, and then it all broke down. I discovered that I didn't like people any more. 1942 was the year they squelched my report, too. I was Assistant D. A., and the D. A. assigned me to investigate the police department here. I and my staff spent eight months on the job and turned in fifteen hundred pages, documenting the abuses and blueprinting the reforms that were needed. Only three men ever saw that report. The D. A., Sanford, and your father. It seemed to me that I was always on the losing side, and I was sick of it. Ten years I had worked for other people, for the public good, and got nowhere. I decided to work for other things—for myself. I decided to become the governor of this state.

"I resigned from the D. A.'s office and ran for the council in 1943. I had a reputation for honesty, and they were afraid of me. They voted unborn babies against me, unnaturalized citizens, two generations of graveyards. They threatened and beat my ward workers, and punched holes in the gasoline tanks of their cars. Your father laughed in my face when I met him after the election. He told me I could never be elected dogcatcher in this town. But he was afraid of me."

"He had reason to be," I said. It was strange to be sitting here talking with the man who killed my father, and stranger still to feel no strong emotion one way or the other. They were simply two men, a cheerful cynic and a solemn cynic, each of them partly good and partly evil, and the more dangerous one had killed the other.

"Not then," Allister protested. "Not in the way you mean. I had no idea of killing him then. I was simply a political threat to him. There are good people in this city, Weather, and they supported me. I was never stronger than the day after the election, when they saw how badly I had lost, and the lengths to which the machine had gone to beat me. The next year the clean government faction drafted me to run for Mayor against Sanford's and your father's candidate. He was a nonentity, but he had the machine behind him, and it was a close campaign. I had a better than even chance of winning, I think, until they got hold of my relation with—her." He twitched his head towards the kitchen. "I made a terrible mistake when I became involved with her."

"Blackmail?"

"Not exactly that—political blackmail. Your father got hold of some of my letters to her." He had lowered his voice so that she wouldn't hear him. "I think her brother stole them, or she may have sold them herself. Anyway, your father was going to publish them, and that would have ended my political life. Don't you see?"

"I see," I answered flatly. "So you ended his instead."

"I'm not trying to justify myself. I'm trying to explain how it happened. It wasn't just the letters. It was the cumulative effect of years of frustration, and they were the last straw. Whenever I moved, he blocked my path. With those letters he was going to shame me before the whole city, the whole state. I couldn't face it."

"You postponed it for a while. Now you have to face something worse, something really final. What happened to the letters after you shot him?"

He glanced at the table. "Those are the letters. I don't know how Kerch got them."

"I think I do," I said, thinking of Floraine Weather.

"You thought you built a trap for J.D., but you were really building one for yourself."

"I realized that the night I killed him. It's been pressed on me every day since then—"

"Yeah. But let's get down to deatils. You're a good shot, so you probably have your own gun. But you were careful not to use it."

"I don't want to talk about it," he said.

"All right. I'll talk. You got hold of a gun that couldn't be connected with you, an old Smith and Wesson revolver, which Joe Sault had picked up in a secondhand store. His sister got you another gun last night, didn't she? It took me a long time to see the connection, but it finally clicked. Once you had the gun, there was the problem of place and time. You studied J.D.'s habits, and found out that he passed the Mack Building every night about the same time. You didn't know that a couple of Kerch's gunmen were making a study of him, too. You laid an ambush for him by breaking into an empty office in the Mack Building. You opened a window above the sidewalk where he always passed, and waited with your gun ready. At that point your plan went wild and the trap for him turned into a trap for both of you."

"Yes," was all he said. His words had run out.

"Kerch's man Garland saw you at the window. Maybe he thought you were somebody my father had hired to gun for him and Rusty Jahnke. Whatever he thought, he came after you. He beat it around the corner to the Mack Street entrance and entered the building to catch you from behind. You must have killed my father before he got to you. Rusty Jahnke, who was driving for him, was still within earshot when the shots were fired. Garland caught you in the office with a smoking gun."

"In the hall. It was a terrible moment—"

"Yeah. A terrible moment that stretched itself out into two years and isn't over yet. Because Garland had a sharp eye for possibilities. He knew who you were and what you had done. He took you to his boss and explained the situation. It must have sounded very lovely to Kerch. He was rid of my father without dirtying his own hands, and he had you and the town where he wanted you. When you won the election and moved into the city hall, you were Kerch's man at the head of Kerch's administration."

"I couldn't help myself," he said in a strangled voice. He looked from side to side of the room as if every door he had passed through in the last two years had shut and locked behind him.

"You didn't have to go through with it. You could have withdrawn from the election. After you won, you still had a chance to resign."

"No. I had to do what he told me. He had the letter he made me write to Judge Simeon. The police found my revolver in the sewer where he planted it. He had Joe Sault and Francie to swear that they had procured it for me—"

"I didn't have anything to do with it!" Mrs. Sontag had come quietly out of the kitchen and was standing in the doorway.

Allister turned on her. "Joe did! He was working for Kerch then."

"Is that why you let him be killed last night? Is that why?"

"I tell you I didn't know—"

"All right," I said loudly. "Kerch had your confession and two witnesses. They weren't good witnesses but they were enough to frighten you badly and permanently. It explains why you were so co-operative with me last night. If you could get somebody else to shoot Kerch, you'd be halfway out of the mess you were in. But you were in too much of a hurry and you repeated your first mistake. You went back to the same source for a gun—to Mrs. Sontag and her brother."

"Try and prove it!" the woman said.

I disregarded her. "For a while after that the situation seemed to be working out in your favor, but all you could do was wait. You were afraid to act until you knew what was going on. It must have been hard to wait and do nothing when Mrs. Sontag gave you my message from the Wildwood Inn."

"Hard on him!" the woman said. "I saw Joey in the morgue a little while ago. He was a handsome boy, but you should see him with dirt in his eyes."

"I saw him."

"And this man let him be killed, didn't you, Allister-Pallister? This morning he had the gall to ask me not to tell you that I gave him the message."

"You were being careful, weren't you?" I said. "You thought you saw a chance for yourself. When I told you Sault was dead, the chance brightened. You beat it out to the Wildwood and found Garland where I left him, unconscious on the kitchen floor. He was the last witness against you, or the second-last, and you strangled him. Then you came back to town and picked up Hanson and went out there again to discover his body.

"That left Kerch. He was the hard one. He had the evidence to burn you locked in his safe at the Cathay Club. Even if you killed him, you couldn't get at the evidence. No wonder your nerves were jumping when I saw you at the police station. When I gave you the combination of that safe, it must have seemed like manna from heaven. It gave you back your confidence, didn't it?"

"Too much," he said dejectedly. "I went too far."

"You went too far years ago. When you went out there to shoot Kerch, you were so far out of touch with the human norm that no living person was safe with you. They were all your enemies. Kerch had to die one way or another, and nobody's going to grieve for him, but after you killed him you made another bad mistake. Carla came downstairs to see what the shooting was about. She was a friend of yours, but all that meant was that she had to die too. Killing people was getting easier and easier—almost enjoyable by now—"

"I don't want to hear any more." There was genuine anguish in his voice, and, for the first time, I felt almost sorry for him. His dream of power had fallen away completely, leaving him naked and pitiful.

"I'm nearly finished," I said, "and so are you. Carla didn't die, Allister. She'll be on the stand at your trial. But you didn't notice that your aim was wild. You gathered up your papers and got out of there. The bullets left in your clip were burning a hole in your pocket. Nearly all your enemies were dead, but Francie was still alive, and she knew enough about you to pin you down. A slug could fix that, though. It was beginning to look as if a slug could fix anything—any problem at all under the sun. So you came to pay a final visit to Francie."

"It's a final visit, all right," she said, "but it isn't final for me. I'll be reading the papers the day you go to the chair. I'll be reading them for laughs."

He was sitting bolt upright, and fits of trembling passed over him in waves which crescendoed and decrescendoed. "Take me away from her," he said.

"When I get ready."

"What are you going to do?"

"I don't know. You shouldn't touch things I care about. If Carla is dead, I'm going to make you suffer."

"I'm suffering now. I've suffered for two years."

"Listen to him!" she jeered. "He used to come crying in my lap like that."

"Shut up!" I realized suddenly that I couldn't do anything to Allister. Nobody could do anything more to him but end his life, and that would probably be doing him a favor.

"This is between him and I," she said.

"I don't think so. But shut up anyway!"

"Aren't you going to call the police?"

"In a minute. Where's his gun?"

She took it out of her pocket and held it out of my reach. "I'm keeping it. I feel safer."

"Keep it, then. Can you handle it?"

"What do you think?"

"Hold it on him. Where's the phone?"

"Beside the kitchen door."

I left them together and called the General Hospital. After some delay Hanson was brought to the phone.

"Weather speaking. I'm in the Harvey Apartments, in Mrs. Sontag's flat. I'll wait here for you."

"Why the hell—?"

"Your man is with me."

"What man?"

"Allister. He's ready to confess my father's murder and a couple of others."

I heard his breath rush into the mouthpiece. "Not Freeman Allister? There must be some mistake."

"There's no mistake. Are you coming? I'm getting bored with his company."

"Right over," he said quickly.

"Don't hang up. How is the girl?"

"I been waiting for her to be able to talk, but she hasn't come to. The doctor says she will any minute. She'll be all right."

"You sure?"

"Yeah, we're taking good care of her."

"What kind of a room is she in?"

"Semiprivate."

"Listen to me! This is important, and I want it done now. Have her moved to a private room with a special nurse—"

"I can't do that. You got to be a relative."

"Do it for me. I'm a relative."

"The hell—"

"I'm going to marry her, see?" I hung up.

The receiver came down with a crash like an explosion. No, the explosion was in the other room. I ran in, and saw Allister on the floor and the woman standing over him. He too had grown a Cyclops eye, a dark red socket in his forehead weeping tears of blood.

I looked from his empty face to the woman's. Her black eyes were burning with triumph. "Well?" she said.

"Murder is as catching as typhoid, isn't it?"

"Self-defense isn't murder," she started to say.

I turned from her abruptly. I felt as if I had already spent hours in the room with the dead man on the floor and his ex-mistress standing over him with the dangling gun in her hand. Five were enough, and six were too many for me. I was sick and tired and old.

I flung open a window and leaned out over the sill. The sickness I had was more than physical, a spiritual sickness that turned the real world crazy at the edges. The street below the window, bare of everything but the dirty leavings of the last snowfall, was undeniably real and solid. But if an army of rats had turned the corner and marched down the street in front of the Harvey Apartments, I would have watched them without a word.

It was an ugly city, too ugly for a girl like Carla. Too ugly even for the men and women that made it what it was, for Kerch and J.D. Weather and his wife, and Allister and Garland and Joe Sault. If Carla and I wanted to make anything of each other—and that would be hard enough—we'd have to get away from this city. When her shoulder healed, I knew she'd be ready to go.

But then I couldn't be sure that I'd be ready. I had a chance to stay and stick in the monster's crop. I was hardly the man for the job, and I couldn't do it alone, and you couldn't build a City of God in the U. S. A. in 1946. But something better could be made than an organism with an appetite for human flesh. A city could be built for people to live in. Before I decided to leave or stay, I'd have to look for the good men who lived here, the J.D. Weathers who still respected the people, the Kaufmans who lived in the real world and not in a stiff old European dream, the Sanfords who had learned their lessons from history, the Allisters who hadn't broken down. Men with a hunger and a willingness to fight for something more than *filet* in their bellies, women in their beds, the champagne bubbles of power expanding in their egos. Ten rounds by myself had beaten me down, but with good men in my corner I could last for seventy-five.

Far down the street a black police sedan roared into sight and hearing. I put both hands on the window ledge and pushed myself back into the room. The woman was still standing by the body.

"He was a strange man," she said. "I often wanted to kill him. Now I've gone and done it."

The gun fell out of her hand and gleamed on the

carpet. A set of brakes shrieked at the curb outside and a car door slammed. When I looked at her face, it was beginning to work with grief, or with some other passion.

ABOUT THE AUTHOR

Ross Macdonald was born near San Francisco in 1915. He was educated in Canadian schools, travelled widely in Europe, and acquired advanced degrees and a Phi Beta Kappa key at the University of Michigan. In 1938 he married a Canadian girl who is now well known as the novelist Margaret Millar. Mr. Macdonald (Kenneth Millar in private life) taught school and later college, and served as communications officer aboard an escort carrier in the Pacific. For over twenty years he has lived in Santa Barbara and written mystery novels about the fascinating and changing society of his native state. He is a past president of the Mystery Writers of America. In 1964 his novel *The Chill* was given a Silver Dagger award by the Crime Writers' Association of Great Britain. Mr. Macdonald's *The Far Side of the Dollar* was named the best crime novel of 1965 by the same organization. *The Moving Target* was made into the highly successful movie *Harper* (1966). *The Goodbye Look* was a national best-seller for more than three months, and *The Underground Man* (1971) even surpassed it in sales and critical acclaim. Mr. Macdonald's hobbies include sailing, bird watching, all-year swimming and literary criticism.

WHODUNIT?

Bantam did! By bringing you these masterful tales of murder, suspense and mystery!

- ☐ POIROT INVESTIGATES
  by Agatha Christie   7887   95¢
- ☐ THE LEVANTER
  by Eric Ambler   7603 $1.50
- ☐ FIVE PIECES OF JADE
  by John Ball   7509   75¢
- ☐ FAR SIDE OF THE DOLLAR
  by Ross Macdonald   6795   95¢
- ☐ THE MOVING TARGET
  by Ross Macdonald   6793   95¢
- ☐ IN THE HEAT OF THE NIGHT
  by John Ball   6675   75¢
- ☐ DEATH IN THE STOCKS
  by Georgette Heyer   5995   95¢
- ☐ BEFORE MIDNIGHT
  by Rex Stout   5951   75¢
- ☐ HOLIDAY FOR MURDER
  by Agatha Christie   5722   75¢
- ☐ DEATH ON THE NILE
  by Agatha Christie   5710   75¢
- ☐ EPITAPH FOR A SPY
  by Eric Ambler   5603   95¢
- ☐ THE INTERCOM CONSPIRACY
  by Eric Ambler   5594   95¢

Buy them at your local bookstore or use this handy coupon for ordering:

Bantam Books, Inc., Dept. BD, 414 East Golf Road, Des Plaines, Ill. 60016

Please send me the books I have checked above. I am enclosing $_____ (please add 25¢ to cover postage and handling). Send check or money order—no cash or C.O.D.'s please.

Mr/Mrs/Miss_____

Address_____

City_____State/Zip_____

BD—9/73

Please allow three weeks for delivery. This offer expires 9/74.

RELAX!

SIT DOWN

and Catch Up On Your Reading!